Drowning

He saw her swimming in the pool. She was doing laps, wearing a black tank suit, her body flashing through the water. Finally, she came up for air.

"Rick!" she said, sounding surprised, and then happy. She splashed water at him. "You scared me!" She splashed more water, then swam away, laughing.

"Hey, come back!" He watched her for a second, then took off his sneakers and dove into the water.

He caught up to her quickly. As she lunged forward to dunk him, he dove under, grabbing her legs to pull her down instead. They wrestled in the water, laughing so hard that it was hard to keep it up. He grabbed her finally, Lonnie struggling in his arms and trying to push his head underwater. Then suddenly, they were kissing, pressing tightly against each other, braced against the tile wall of the pool. They couldn't get close enough and the kissing was more frantic, arms, hands, and legs twisting together. Mouths and ears and hair.

Other Point paperbacks you will enjoy:

The Edge
  by Jeanne Betancourt

Slumber Party
  by Christopher Pike

Halfway Down Paddy Lane
  by Jean Marzollo

Love Always, Blue
  by Mary Pope Osborne

When We First Met
  by Norma Fox Mazer

SURVIVING

A novelization by
Elizabeth Faucher.

Based on the
television motion
picture written by
Joyce Eliason

SCHOLASTIC INC.
New York Toronto London Auckland Sydney

ISBN 0-590-43731-3

12 11 10 9 8 7 6 5 4 3 2 1   0 1 2 3/9

SURVIVING

Chapter 1

It was sunny, but not really. Not that it rained very often in Santa Barbara, but sometimes — maybe it was just smog on its way over from Los Angeles — sometimes the sky seemed a lot grayer than California sky should be.

Rick probably wasn't late, but just in case, he shrugged to adjust the weight of his knapsack and gave his Yamaha a little more gas, neatly steering out of the way of a eucalyptus branch by the curb. His parents were having a barbecue and they would be expecting him. Spending every hour of free time in the library made it easy to forget that it was summer. But if he didn't pass that honors exam, his father would — Rick shook his head, turning up the volume on his tape deck to block out the thought of failing. Failing. If he failed, he would feel — he turned the volume up higher. Mozart's *Don Giovanni*. Wonderful music. He'd rigged two little stereo speakers onto his handlebars and the sound was great.

There were lots of cars parked in the driveway and in front of the house — the barbecue must have started already — and he swerved in among them, manuevering the scooter as he would a pair of skis on a mogul-crowded slope. He turned into a quick stop and jumped off, popping *Don Giovanni* out of the tape deck and heading for the house.

His mother, Tina, was standing in the hallway, hands on her hips, her legs very tan in shorts. Students of various ethnic backgrounds — she was a counselor for the university foreign exchange programs — were passing her, with trays of food and drinks, on their way to the patio, and Rick had a momentary image of his mother as a traffic cop, working clogged California arteries.

"Take the quesadilla out while it's hot," Tina called to the kitchen. "Oh, and the nachos. Don't let them sit on the counter getting cold." She saw Rick and gave him a distracted smile. "Rick." She gestured toward the student standing shyly next to her. "This is Mitsu Kawabata."

Rick put out his hand; the boy shook it uncertainly. "Nice to meet you."

"Mitsu is going to UC Santa Barbara this year," his mother explained.

"Great," Rick said, and both he and Mitsu nodded. How many of these shy students had he met over the years? He nodded again and turned to go upstairs.

"You're not going to wear that shirt, are you?" Tina asked.

Rick glanced down at his old "No Nukes Is Good Nukes" T-shirt. "What, you don't like my —" No point in arguing. He turned again to go upstairs.

"Oh, and Rick," his mother said after him. "Be nice to Lonnie. She just got home."

Lonnie. His parents' best friends' daughter. "I'm always nice to Lonnie."

"Be *extra* nice," Tina said, rescuing an unwieldy tray from a girl who was trying to carry two and indicating for Mitsu to follow her outside. She managed not to stumble over Ralph, their German shepherd. "Ralph, will you get out of the way?" she asked, bending down to pat him on the head with her free hand. She straightened, opening the sliding glass door to the patio and ushering Mitsu outside. "Now just make yourself at home. Just friends and family." She patted him encouragingly on the shoulder, then carried the tray over to one of the picnic tables.

Upstairs, Rick went into his room, dumping the knapsack on his bed and crossing to his stereo. He put *Don Giovanni* into the tape deck, adjusted the equalizer, then closed the door to the closet his father had helped him convert to a darkroom. The door shouldn't be open — his little brother, Philip, had probably been poking around in there again. He walked back to his bed, taking his books out of his knapsack and placing them on the text-book shelf above his desk.

"Oheehhoooeehaah!" Philip sang from the doorway, trying to make a fourteen-year-old voice sound like Caruso. "Oheehstupeedoh!"

Rick laughed, throwing a pillow at him. The party was getting louder and he moved to the window, picking up a camera and studying the backyard through the lens.

"How do you listen to that junk?" Philip asked, bouncing the pillow off his brother's back.

"I like it," Rick said, scanning the back-yard through the lens. There were a good fifty people there, mostly hanging around the grill for hamburgers, a few of the kids swimming in the pool. He focused on his father, David, handsome and healthy-looking, waited for him to grin, then clicked the shutter.

"You're like, so weird," Philip said, read-justing the equalizer to bring out what little bass there was.

"When you're older, son," Rick said in an extra-deep voice. A lot like his father's voice. His father was giving his mother a bear hug and Rick snapped a picture. "You'll appreci-ate it when you're older."

"No way," Philip said. "Me, and Artie, and the guys're going to —"

"Guess what, Rick!" Their little sister, Sarah, ran in. "Lonnie's here!"

Rick moved the camera, looking for Lonnie and her parents, Lois and Harvey.

"Where is she?" Philip asked, at the window now.

"There!" Sarah pointed, squirming in between them. "With her mom and dad."

Rick found them through the camera, stopping on Lois and Harvey first, then finding Lonnie behind them. She was very thin and pale — in contrast to the tanned, healthy people around her — and her hair seemed even redder than usual. She was shifting her weight from one old Ked to the other, her hands uncomfortable fists in front of her.

"I saw her scars," Sarah said. "They were *gross*. Big, red scars."

Rick automatically moved the camera down toward her hands, then up to her face. Big eyes. Forest animal eyes. His father moved into the picture, grabbing Lonnie in his usual bear hug. Rick clicked his camera.

"Hey, come on, you guys," Sarah said, punching him on the back. "Let's go out there!"

"Yeah, absolutely," Philip said, halfway to the door, already unbuttoning his shirt in preparation for the pool.

Rick lowered his camera and sat at the desk, opening his biology book.

"Rick!" Sarah said. "You can't read *now*."

Rick sighed. Somehow, he just didn't feel up to a whole lot of socializing. Even if he hadn't seen Lonnie since —

"Come on!" Sarah said, trying to pull him out of the chair, too small to have much effect.

"Okay, okay," he said and stood up. "Give me a couple of minutes to change."

"If you don't come down, I'll —"

"I'll be down in a minute," he said. "I promise."

He changed into less ragged jeans and a fairly new UCSB T-shirt and started downstairs, hesitating and going back to get a camera. He always felt more secure with a camera. Besides, his parents and Lonnie's parents were always really into posing for pictures. Like people out of *The Four Seasons* or something.

Indeed, once he got outside, he became Resident Photographer.

"Another one, Rick," his father said, slinging one arm around Harvey, the other around Tina; Harvey's arm was around Lois. "Have to get my best side here," he said to Harvey, who laughed.

Cooperatively, Rick snapped the picture. Harvey and his father had been friends since they were in elementary school. Harvey was a big, burly guy, his face and stomach showing the regular beers the two men had together a lot more than David's did. David always looked great, like he had just stepped off a tennis court — even when he had just stepped out of the operating room. Rick had always hoped that when *he* was his father's age, he would be —

"One more, Rick," his mother said, moving to pose with Lois.

Rick took the picture, noticing the other contrast. Lois was heavily into beads, macrame, and makeup. His mother was more the simple silver-chain-and-pearl-earrings type.

"This is what it's all about," David said. "Good friends, family. . . ."

Tina laughed. "Oh, no, here comes the love and honor speech."

David laughed, too. "Most important things in the world." He pointed at Rick. "And don't you forget it. Love, and honor, and — good credit!"

"Good old David," Lois said, fumbling in her skirt pocket for a piece of Kleenex and rubbing her teeth with it. She leaned toward Tina. "I didn't have lipstick on my teeth, did I?"

"No," Tina said. "I think it was eyeshadow."

The women exchanged smiles, then Lois moved to take Rick's arm.

"Let's go find Lonnie," she said. "You can make her smile. I'm sure you can." She hugged him, Rick responding self-consciously. His parents and the Carlsons did a lot of hugging. As she pulled him over to the pool, David caught up and clapped him on the shoulder.

"You were late," he said. "Where've you been all afternoon?"

"At the library. Studying."

"Good boy." David turned to Lois. "Tina

tell you? Rick's trying to get into the honors science program at the university. *Fifteen* students will be selected out of a hundred —"

Lois laughed. "She told me! Three times!"

"I, uh, I have to pass the test first," Rick said, flushing.

"You'll pass the test," David said confidently and paused to think for a second. "Altruism."

Rick kicked at the grass, flushing more. "Dad, come on."

"*You* come on," his father said, grinning. "Altruism."

Rick sighed. "Selflessness. Doing stuff for other people without personal gain."

"Epicene."

Rick managed to smile back, being a good sport. "Uh, having both male and female characteristics."

As his father started to say another test word, Lois moved in between them. "David, get off the kid's back — it's a party." She took Rick's arm. "Does he ever give you a day off?"

Rick shrugged, embarrassed.

Lonnie was over by the pool, lying on a lounge chair near the trees. She had taken off her jeans and long-sleeved shirt and was wearing a light yellow bikini that still seemed dark against her skin. Her eyes were closed in the sunlight and Rick noticed how peaceful she looked. Relaxed. Beautiful.

"Lonnie?" Lois said. "Surprise. . . ."

Lonnie flinched, her eyes opening abruptly. Seeing Rick, her face relaxed into a smile.

Lois laughed, nudging him. "Did I tell you?"

"Uh, hi," Rick said, hands going into his pockets. "Tulip."

Lois reached down, moving the hair out of Lonnie's face. "I knew he could make you smile."

"Mama," Lonnie said impatiently, brushing her mother's hand away. Shyly, she looked at Rick. "You grew!"

He blushed. "So did you."

Neither of them could think of anything else to say, and Lois laughed.

"I'll tell you," she started. "You two —"

"He's not as tall as his old dad yet," David said, having heard the end of the conversation. "Let's hit the pool, guys — it's the over-the-hill-gang against the punks!"

The pool was large, but soon almost everyone had crowded into the water and a wild volleyball game started. Some of Rick's friends from school, guys he hadn't seen much this summer, had shown up. He and Bobby had played on a lot of different teams, and Jeb — well, Jeb wasn't exactly athletic, but he had always been a buddy. It was a little weird seeing them after spending so much time buried in books this summer. But, if he didn't study, his father — Rick looked across the little net at David diving past Harvey at the ball, knocking it over the net.

All those years of being friends, and he and Harvey still competed like crazy, Harvey *still* trying to measure up. Jeb was kind of like that sometimes.

The ball bounced high on their side and Lonnie hit it to him; Rick smashed it over the net; Harvey missed the shot.

"Hey, Harvey, you're getting old!" David said, grinning. "Not moving the way you used to."

"What are you talking about?" Harvey asked. "I *never* moved good!" He looked at Rick, gesturing toward David. "I need this from my best friend, right? Been needling me all my life."

"Who, me?" David asked, all innocence.

Rick smiled at Lonnie. "Good shot, Tulip."

She smiled back. "You always call me that. My name isn't Tulip."

He winked at her, glancing over his shoulder at Philip's closest, and twerpiest, friend Artie, who was straightening his glasses and winding up a skinny right arm to serve the ball.

Philip swooped underwater, grabbing Artie's legs and playfully dunking him.

"Hey!" Artie came up, coughing. "My glasses!" He splashed around, looking for them. "Hey, where are they?" He splashed more frantically, not aware that they had washed up on top of his head.

Philip laughed. "You lost 'em, Four Eyes."

Rick, also laughing, stopped as he saw that Artie was really panicked. "Hey," he pushed his brother. "Don't be a jerk." He made his way over to Artie, moving the glasses down over his eyes. "You okay?"

Artie flushed, wiping the water off the lenses. "I just — I don't want to lose my glasses."

"I don't blame you," Rick said. "You look good in them." He glanced over at Lonnie, aware that she was smiling at him, and smiled back.

Chapter 2

The party went on for a long time. As it got darker, Tina put Fifties rock and roll on the stereo, and danced on the patio with her husband. Harvey and Lois were dancing, too, and Rick watched them, noticing that Lonnie was off under the trees, sitting on the grass, away from the party. He crossed the patio with enough food to keep Bobby and Jeb busy for a while, seeing that they were also looking at Lonnie.

"I was just telling Jeb that stuff I heard about her," Bobby said, as Rick sat down next to them.

"Hey, come on," Rick said. "She's had a lot of trouble."

"Yeah, but it's true," Bobby said. "Boyd Henrie was one of the guys."

"I said, cut it out!" Rick scowled at them, put the plates o nthe grass, and walked over toward the trees. "Hi," he said.

Lonnie's smile was shy. "My mother," she said, sounding embarrassed. "I could just die. She always tries to act so 'groovy.' " She covered her eyes. "This is *embarrassing*."

Rick looked at the patio. His mother and Lois were dancing together, very energetic, now looking like the Sixties Revisited. He laughed. "Come on. They're good dancers."

"Oh, yeah," Lonnie said. She lay back on the grass, focusing on the sky. "I'm exhausted." She shook her head. "I forgot about these parties."

Rick nodded, sitting down next to her. His parents weren't famous for parties that broke up early.

Lonnie lifted herself onto one elbow. "I saw you over there with Bobby. Is he still your best friend?"

"Kind of. I mean, I guess." He ran his hand back through his hair. His father would be after him to have it trimmed soon. "I don't know — we don't have too much in common anymore."

Lonnie tilted her head. "What do you mean?"

"I don't know. We're interested in kind of different things." He looked over at Bobby and Jeb, who were laughing about something and being rowdy with Philip. "Anyway, I'm busy. I've been working in my dad's office. Computerizing his records."

Lonnie sat up, taking a nacho from the plate next to her on the grass, moving it so Rick could have some, too. "Are you going to be a doctor?"

Rick hesitated and took a nacho. "Dad

thinks I am — he's already training me. He says medicine can be my meal ticket." He laughed. "What *I* want is to be a photographer. Some meal ticket."

Lonnie laughed, too, and as she picked up her napkin, Rick couldn't help noticing her wrist. She saw him looking and slowly turned her hand so he could see the jagged red scars. "You can see if you want."

"No." Quickly, Rick looked away. "I wasn't —"

"I want to talk about it and nobody will!" Lonnie shook her head, her voice less controlled. "When I got out of the hospital, and I was coming home, I was so happy. I kept thinking that Mama and Daddy would *have* to talk about it. They'd *have* to listen. Only," she shook her head again, managing a weak laugh, "they never said a word. About what happened, about what it was like being in a hospital all those months. All they talked about on the way home from the airport was their T-shirt business, and how the weather's changing, and this might be the beginning of the ice age. . . ." Lonnie laughed again, more bitterly.

"Why —" Rick hesitated. "Why'd you — do it?"

"I thought I might as well get it over with," she said quietly.

"Get what over with?"

"Well — we're all going to die *anyway*, Rick." She studied the insides of her wrists. "I cut 'em wrong, though. If I'd done it right,

I'd be dead already." Her fists tightened. "I kept goofing up, and getting in deeper, and — I just wanted to stop." She glanced up. "Haven't you ever felt that way? Like it's not worth the effort?"

He nodded slowly. "Yeah. Sometimes." He coughed, breaking the spell. "But, you have to keep going, trying —"

"Who says?" Lonnie asked. "Anyway, it didn't matter. I can never do anything right. I couldn't even *kill* myself right."

It was quiet for a second.

"Well," Rick reached out to touch her arm, very awkward. "I'm glad you didn't."

Lonnie looked back at him, her face breaking into one of the happiest smiles he had ever seen.

On the patio, dancing, Tina watched Rick and Lonnie talking. She nudged Lois.

"She looks good," Tina said. "Happy."

Lois followed her eyes. "Do you think so?"

Tina nodded. "The worst is over. She was just going through a phase."

It was later, and Rick and Lonnie were up in his room, listening to *The Magic Flute*. Sarah had shown up with bowls of ice cream, hanging out on the bed with Lonnie while Rick looked through his records, trying to decide what to play next.

"Pamina is telling him she'll always be by his side," he said as the passage was ending. "And how the magic flute will protect them."

Sarah yawned. "Do you like heavy metal?"

she asked Lonnie, who shrugged affirmatively. "Well, then, wait." Sarah got off the bed. "I've got this one album, the Death Squad. You wanna hear it?" She headed for the door without waiting for an answer.

When she was gone, Lonnie put her ice-cream bowl on the bedside table. "I think your little sister is afraid I'm going to take you away from her," she said, her laugh shy.

"Oh, yeah," Rick said, reddening. "You better watch it."

"*You* watch it."

He grinned, making a grab for her sneaker, Lonnie rolling nimbly out of the way. Without thinking about it, they started to wrestle, the way they always had, each struggling to pin the other.

"Hey, Tulip," Rick said, out of breath. "You're pretty ferocious!"

Lonnie laughed, struggling away from him. "Don't call me that!"

They both laughed, stopping suddenly as they realized how close they were.

"I thought about you," Lonnie said quietly. "When I was in the hospital. . . ." She smiled. "I kept thinking about those dumb plays we used to put on in our garage."

"They weren't dumb," Rick said. "*I* wrote them."

Lonnie giggled. "Remember the one about the baby from outer space?" Her smile faded and she reached out to touch his shoulder. "I had such a crush on you. You never even looked at me — I was such a little runt."

"That's because every time I looked at you, it made you cry," Rick said, teasing.

"I was shy. See, I — I loved you." She hesitated. "I was a pretty dumb little kid."

The music was louder, even more beautiful, and they looked at each other. Slowly, Lonnie let her hand touch Rick's face, then both hands, then kissed him, very quickly.

Sarah hurried back in, stopped, and then continued over to the bed. She sat down, grabbing her ice cream and taking a bite. "Your ice cream's melting," she said, very nonchalant.

Rick coughed and stood up, moving his hand through his hair to straighten it. "I, uh — you guys wanna see some stars?" He turned off the light, then flipped another switch, stars lighting up across the dark ceiling, glittering as though they really were outside.

"I see the Big Dipper," Lonnie said, sounding awed.

"Yeah, uh," Rick shifted his weight, not sure if they would be able to see him pointing in the darkness. "There's Ursa Major, the great bear, Cetus, the whale —"

Sarah groaned. "Stop being *smart*!"

Outside, Philip, Artie, and a couple of boys from the neighborhood were playing football in the darkness while David and Tina cleaned up, Harvey and Lois helping them. Everyone else had gone.

"Okay, Philip," Tina said, bundling up a tablecloth. "Party's over."

"In a minute," he called back, ball tucked under one arm, dodging past the other boys.

"Philip's getting to be quite an athlete," Harvey remarked as David folded up the last of the rental chairs.

David nodded. "He's okay. He doesn't have the natural ability Rick has. I don't think he has the desire either."

"Well," Harvey said, very good-natured, "we all know Rick's perfect."

Tina shook her head. "Rick's got his own problems. Last year, he had a million kids here every day. This summer, it's stopped."

"Well, he's finally applying himself," David said.

"He still needs friends. Everybody needs friends."

"He's got friends," David said impatiently. "Right now, he just has other priorities."

Harvey jumped in. "Tell you what. I'll trade *our* problems for your problems."

The two couples walked to the door, David's arm around Tina.

"It was great," Lois said. "As usual." She shook her head as they went inside, the house comfortable and cluttered, but much neater than a house should be two hours after a large party. "I don't know how you do it, Tina." She stopped at the bottom of the stairs. "Lonnie? We're going."

"So," David said to Harvey. "How about some racquetball tomorrow? Early."

"I hate getting slaughtered first thing in the morning." Harvey grinned. "Call me."

Lonnie appeared with Sarah, Rick right behind them. She looked back at him, smiling. "Good-night, Rick."

He blushed. "Good-night, Tulip."

They kept smiling at each other and, at the bottom of the stairs, Tina frowned slightly.

"Lonnie, stand up straight," Lois said.

Lonnie sighed and came downstairs. "I *am*, Mama."

The beeper on David's belt went off and he groaned. "Not again," he said, heading for the phone.

"It was too good to be true," Tina said. "A whole day without a call from the hospital."

Harvey laughed, holding the front door as Lois and Lonnie went outside. "No rest for the wicked."

Rick hung around near the door until he heard the Carlsons' car pull away, then went to the den to see if his father might let him come along to the hospital.

"I'll be right over," his father was saying quietly, almost whispering. He checked his watch. "Ten minutes. Right." Seeing Rick, he hung up.

"Can I go with you?"

"Uh, no, not this time." David cleared his throat. "It's going to be a long night. Sounds like I have to operate."

Rick nodded, disappointed, but not surprised.

* * *

Tina sat at the piano, working on a Brahms concerto. She had been a concert pianist, before, and still spent a good deal of her time practicing. Philip and Sarah slouched on the sofa, half listening, laughing as they looked at Sarah's newest Death Squad album.

"These guys're almost as good as Twisted Sister," Philip said, making a face to imitate the lead singer on one of the album covers. "Look at that one — throat cut, teeth hanging out, blood and pus —"

"Philip!" Sarah shrieked.

"Like that excellent video. With the blood dripping, vampires coming after him, ripping —"

"Quiet from the peanut gallery," Tina said, not turning away from the piano. "I'm practicing."

Philip slouched down, briefly, then couldn't resist making an even worse face at Sarah, reaching out for her with clawlike hands. Just as he reached her throat, Sarah screamed; their mother groaned and played more loudly to drown them out.

It was late, but Rick wasn't tired and he stayed in his darkroom, developing the pictures he'd taken at the party, watching a large, smiling picture of Lonnie appear on the paper in the developing fluid. When each image sharpened, he pinned the picture up to dry and went on to the next, working with practiced care.

When the pictures were dry, he spread them out on his desk, studying each with a magnifying glass, studying the ones of Lonnie the longest.

He ended up with one in each hand: Lonnie smiling, making a happy clown face for the camera, for him; Lonnie sitting alone on the grass, arms hugging herself, her eyes afraid and despairing. He looked from one to the other, intrigued by the two sides of her personality. Fascinated. *Attracted.*

Chapter 3

The morning sunlight was especially bright in Lonnie's room, almost hurting her eyes as it bounced off the newly painted white walls and furniture. She patted her kitten, Timmy, while Lois sat on the edge of the bed, moving the hair away from her eyes.

"We have to get this cut," her mother said. "You look like a wild gypsy."

Lonnie patted Timmy.

"You start your dancing lessons on Tuesday," Lois went on. "It'll help you with your posture. You ever notice how beautifully dancers carry themselves?"

Lonnie groaned. "I don't *want* to take dancing lessons."

"Don't be silly, it'll be fun," Lois said. "And Mimi called. She's dying to see you."

Lonnie made a face. "She's boring. All she talks about is Boy George."

Lois ignored that, kissing her on the forehead and standing up. "Daddy's waiting — I have to go. Alma will fix you some breakfast."

Lonnie sat up. "Mama? Can I paint my room black?"

"Lonnie, we just painted it white," Lois said, exasperated. "You *wanted* it white."

"I saw this room in a magazine. It had black sheets, and black towels —"

"The answer is *no*," Lois said. "You cannot paint this room black. We had it all fixed up for you."

Lonnie looked around at the white dresser, the white desk, the white rocking chair. "It's corny."

Lois opened the door. "Good-bye, Lonnie."

"Can I go with you?"

Lois turned, surprised. "To work?"

"Yeah." Lonnie jumped off the bed. "Please?"

"There's nothing for you to do down there —"

"Wait," Lonnie hurried into the bathroom, "I just have to wash my face."

Lois leaned against the doorjamb, completely baffled. Sometimes Lonnie was capable of — she shook her head. "You'll be *bored*," she said.

Before going to the medical center, David and Rick went down to the beach for a swim.

"You've got it made," David said, jogging toward the water. "A swim in the Pacific every morning. When I was a kid, I had to get up at 5 A.M. to deliver papers!" He ran faster. "Come on, Rick. You going to let me beat you?"

Rick picked up the pace, fighting to stay even. "Maybe I'm not as good as you are."

"I don't expect you to be as good as I am," David shouted, almost at the water. "I expect you to be *better*!" He dove in, and Rick dove after him — both swimming hard, battling each other even more than they were battling the waves.

At the office, Rick went through a box of slides, checking the labels against the list in his lap, making sure everything was in order for his father's lecture that afternoon. David sat at the desk, sifting through papers. The office decor was quiet and tasteful, mostly Art Deco.

"Okay, Dad. Let's rehearse." Rick held a slide up to the light. "This one is MacFarland."

"Subdural hematoma," his father said automatically. "The patient fell and hit her head, formed a blood clot."

Rick nodded, taking out another slide. "What about Dimmick?"

"Uh . . ." David frowned. "Dimmick?"

"Meningioma," Rick prompted him.

"Oh, yeah. A benign tumor. But, in the brain, anything that takes up space can cause pressure." He paused. "Don't go out for neurosurgery, Rick. It's too depressing. We know so damned little about the brain." He shook his head. "Surgery's a gross specialty. Maybe . . . pediatrics."

"Well, I don't know if I'd be good," Rick said hesitantly. "You know. With patients and stuff."

"Patients are easy," David said. "All you have to do is establish physical contact. Touch a shoulder, a hand, an arm. It reassures them, gives them confidence. Calms them down."

May, his nurse, bustled in, brisk and no-nonsense. "You've got one in there now, waiting to be calmed down," she said quietly.

David headed for the door, papers forgotten. "I'll be right back," he said to Rick.

May followed him. "You've got a meeting with the surgical staff after the lecture this afternoon."

David sighed. "I'm going to need astral projection to get there."

Rick watched them go, partially sympathetic, even more admiring. He spent most of the morning at the computer, entering patients' charts. May was in and out, adding charts to the stack.

"Where are you?" she asked, depositing a few more.

Rick looked up from the terminal, blinking to focus. "The 'L's.' Lovell, Margaret."

May shook her head. "You work so hard. You ever goof off?"

Rick grinned sheepishly, going on to the next chart.

"Your father thinks he's got a sixteen-year-old intern here." May clicked her tongue, very disapproving. "It's summer, you should be having some fun. A good-looking kid like you. . . . You got a girl friend?"

Rick laughed. "No."

"You should have a girl friend." She nodded, then lifted a stack of finished charts.

"Here." Rick jumped up to help her. "Let me give you a hand."

They were carrying the charts back to the files when a woman burst out of one of the examining rooms, and started down the hall. She was attractive — tall and thin, wearing jeans and a big, floppy sweater. David hurried out of the room after her.

"Wait," he said, saw Rick, and stopped, noticeably paling.

The woman didn't pause, the main door slamming after her as she left the reception room. David turned, going into his office, and Rick hesitated before following May into the records room. She got there ahead of him, grimly filing charts.

"Who was that?" Rick asked. "That woman?"

"Nobody," May said quickly. "I mean — she's just —" She blinked several times. "You know, Rick, you should take a day and just go to the beach and lie in the sun." She turned back to the files, shoving the charts into their places.

Rick frowned for a second, confused, but recovered himself and moved to help her.

* * *

Later, he walked with his father to the lecture room, lugging the box of slides.

"Dad?" He shifted the box to his other arm. "Who was that woman?"

His father's pace quickened. "What woman?"

"That real pretty woman. The one who was so angry."

"I don't know who you're talking about — hey, you've got all the slides?"

Rick nodded. Hadn't his father noticed that he'd spent an hour organizing them? "Yeah, they're all lined up."

"Good boy." His father's expression relaxed and he slung his arm around Rick's shoulders. "Epistemology."

Not again. Yeah, again. Rick let out his breath, not quite sighing. "A study of the origin of knowledge."

"You're getting good." David looked at the ceiling, thinking. "Here's one for you. Ochlocracy."

"What?"

"Ochlocracy. Government by the mob. Mob rule." He moved his jaw. "You gonna hit the books today, Rick?"

"Well — I was kind of thinking about going to the beach."

David winced. "Do me a favor. Go to the library, get ready for your exam. Success ultimately depends on how you use your time."

Rick nodded, his shoulders slumping.

"Besides, too much sun isn't good for you, anyway."

Rick nodded again. The box of slides felt a whole lot heavier than it had before.

Naturally, once they got to the factory, Lonnie was bored. She wandered around her mother's office, looking at T-shirt samples, at new designs on the drawing board, at a coffee stain on the edge of her mother's desk. Lois was on the phone, bawling someone or other out.

"The neck's wrong," she was saying. "The ribbing pulls. There's no way to fix it. We're going to have to *eat* three thousand shirts!"

Completely uninterested, Lonnie wandered down to the shipping room. She watched the men pack boxes for a while, then joined in.

"Hey!" her father said. "What are you doing?"

She glanced up from the order form she was filling, seeing Harvey coming down the aisle, the workers moving to let him past.

"Helping," she said, holding the order form in one hand, some shirts in the plastic envelopes in the other.

Harvey smiled stiffly, bending down next to her. "It's — it's distracting," he said. "Having a pretty young girl in here. . . . You understand. . . ."

Lonnie jumped up. "That's ridiculous! I'm a hard worker!" She realized that everyone could hear them and lowered her voice. "I wasn't flirting — you always think that. You never trust me!"

"Look." Harvey took her arm, also aware of the men working around them and over-hearing the conversation. "You wanna work? I'll give you some work."

Lonnie jerked free. "I don't want to type your stupid Rolodex cards! I just —" Why did this always have to happen? Why couldn't he, for *once*, let her do something she wanted? "I just —" She could feel her face flushing, tears heating up in her eyes. "I just want to go home." She hurried down the aisle toward the exit, trembling, barely able to keep from running.

Chapter 4

During his father's lecture, Rick manned the slide projector. David nodded for him to start and Rick clicked the first slide into place, a large close-up of a brain.

"Hi," David said, smiling at the audience of interns. "My name's Richard Pryor."

Everyone laughed and Rick felt a surge of pride.

"Somewhere in this 'squash,'" David gestured toward the slide, "this mass of cells, is a *Hamlet*. A *Macbeth*. Or maybe a *My Fair Lady*."

More laughter. Rick beamed, but recovered his concentration quickly as his father motioned for him to click to the next slide.

"Somewhere," David said, "inside this bony covering, there's a connection between the mind and the brain. Nobody's ever seen it. Nobody's ever defined it. We, as surgeons, probe. . . ."

After the lecture, Rick had to wait to get through to his father as interns crowded around, asking questions. When the last one finally left, Rick hurried over.

"Dad," he started, "that was really —"

"Did you get all the slides?" David asked.

"Uh — well, yeah, I will." Rick moved to the projector. "Your speech was really good."

David shrugged. "Well, if you give enough of them. . . ." He glanced at his watch. "I'm going to be tied up for the rest of the afternoon. You heading for the library?"

"Well — I mean, yeah, I guess so."

"Good boy," David said. "Do me a favor and take the slides back to my office, and then I'll see you tonight."

Rick nodded.

The library was almost empty and Rick tried to concentrate on his books, instead of the sun streaming through the windows. The beach was probably — he stared at a diagram of a double helix. A boy and a girl about his age were sitting across from him, whispering to each other. The girl had a magazine open, but the boy would whisper something and she would giggle. His hand was on her shoulder, very tanned against her white halter, and Rick shifted in his seat, trying to study. Now the girl leaned over to give the boy a swift kiss and there was more whispering.

Rick let his hand drift over to his notebook, opening to the picture of Lonnie he'd put between the pages. A thoughtful pose, her knees drawn up, arms wrapped around them, head tilted as she looked at something far away. Rick studied the picture, hearing the couple across the table laugh and whisper. More laughing. The sound of another kiss.

Abruptly, he closed the notebook, shoved it into his knapsack, and got up from the table. The couple didn't even blink.

As he steered his scooter into her driveway, he saw her swimming in the pool. She was doing laps, wearing a black tank suit, her body flashing through the water. He let the bike fall, and crossed the lawn to the pool.

Swimming hard, she didn't notice him and he waited at one end, grinning down at her when she came up for air.

"Rick!" she said, sounding surprised, and then happy. She splashed water at him with one palm. "You scared me!" She splashed more water, then swam away, laughing.

"Hey, come back!" He watched her for a second, then took off his sneakers and dove into the water.

He caught up to her quickly and she splashed more water at him; Rick laughing and splashing back. As she lunged forward to dunk him, he dove under, grabbing her legs to pull her down instead. They wrestled in the water, laughing so hard that it was hard to keep it up. He grabbed her finally, Lonnie struggling in his arms and trying to push his head underwater. Then suddenly, they were kissing, pressing tightly against each other, braced against the tile wall of the pool. They couldn't get close enough and the kissing was more frantic, arms, hands, and legs twisting together. Mouths and ears and hair.

It was later and Lonnie stood in the hall of the kitchen, her suit dripping water on the floor. Alma, their maid, was at the kitchen table, drinking coffee.

"Alma," Lonnie said, being casual, "you might as well go on home."

Alma considered that, mug in hand. "Is all right?" she asked, and Lonnie nodded. "You are sure?"

"Positive."

"Well." Alma stood up, draining the last of the coffee. "Then I go." She took her handbag from the counter. "I do my grocery shopping."

Lonnie smiled and nodded.

"Good-bye for now, Lonnie."

"Bye." As soon as the kitchen door closed, Lonnie turned and looked down the hall at Rick, who was also dripping water.

"Okay?" he asked.

She nodded and he came down the hall.

"I'm, uh" — he looked at the floor — "kind of —"

"I'll get some towels," she said, moving past him.

"Tulip."

She paused, then giggled. "Don't," she punched his shoulder playfully, "call me that!" She darted away, Rick right behind her, both of them slipping on the water.

Then they were wrestling again, each laughing in the same nervous, out-of-breath way. Laughing too hard to struggle, Lonnie fell onto the stairs, Rick collapsing on top of her.

"Rick!" she said, still laughing, the wrestling still a game.

His smile faded and he reached out to touch her cheek. "You're so pretty...."

"I'm not." She ducked out of the way. "I hate my face." Embarrassed, she scrambled up the stairs, Rick pulling her back down.

"You're beautiful!" he said. "The most beautiful —" He kissed her, pulling her clumsily onto his lap as she threw her arms around his neck, pressing close, and closer. "Don't you know that?" he asked against her mouth. "Don't you know how beautiful —" But now they were kissing too hard to speak, the passion from the pool starting all over again, twice as strong, twice as hard, twice as desperate.

Slowly, Rick pulled his scooter into his driveway, missing her already. The bike had seemed sluggish all the way home, as though he were being pulled back to her house no matter how fast he drove.

"Hey, Rick!"

He turned, seeing Bobby in his old rebuilt Cadillac with Jeb and some other guys. The guys. Somehow he just didn't feel like being with the guys.

"What's happening, Rick?" Bobby asked.

Slowly, Rick walked down the driveway. "Not . . . much."

"You wanna come with us? We're headin' down to the arcade."

"No, I — I've got some stuff I have to do."

"You geek!" Jeb said, hanging out the window. "That's what you *always* say."

"Hey, come on, Rick," Bobby said. "We won't stay long." Rick shook his head, wishing that he had gotten home five minutes earlier, or five minutes later. . . .

"Guess who put it to Sherry Loring?" Jeb asked, the boys in the back laughing.

Rick managed a feeble, half-interested smile.

Jeb pointed at Bobby. "Got her in the backseat."

"Hey, Jeb." Bobby flushed as one of the guys whistled. "Will you guys cut it out?"

"She was all *over* him," Jeb said, more loudly, obviously enjoying this. "She's an animal. Her footprint is still on the *window*."

The guys in the back were all laughing, Bobby not meeting Rick's eyes.

"Yeah," Rick said, backing up. "Well, listen, I — I gotta go, okay?" He headed for the house, not waiting for their reactions. Had he been like that before? Rowdy, and laughing, and — it seemed like a long time ago. Like, when he was a lot younger. A *lot* younger.

He sat in his room, leaning with his back against the side of the bed, grinning foolishly as he looked up at his stars. He had called her right after dinner and now, as they talked, he couldn't remember if it had been a couple of minutes or a couple of hours.

"Me?" he asked, his voice soft. "I mostly like chocolate ice cream. Actually, anything chocolate. . . ."

Lonnie, at her house, had gone into her bathroom and closed the door — the only place she was sure they would leave her alone. "What about potatoes?" she asked. "Baked potatoes with sour cream and chives. . . ."

"Mmmmm," he said.

"You know what was gross? The food at the hospital."

He nodded, even though she couldn't see him.

"They work to try and make you feel better about yourself, but," she found herself smiling at the illogic, "the food is nothing but starch. So if you eat, you gain all this weight, and then you feel terrible about yourself all over again. . . ."

They laughed quietly, privately.

"Anyway," Lonnie said. "I never ate very much. I wasn't hungry." She swallowed. "Rick? I don't know anything. Opera, literature — you're practically a *genius* and I . . . flunked out." She swallowed again, the old panic bubbling up. "I'm so scared, Rick, about going back. I mean, when school starts." She gulped. "Y-you know about me, don't you? I mean, you've heard things?"

Rick picked up a pencil, rolling it in his

hand, letting it snap. "I, uh — whatever you've done is okay."

"Rick," Lonnie clenched her free hand, rocking back and forth on the edge of the tub. "You're the only one — who means anything, you —" She took a couple of deep breaths, trembling, the panic back, worse than ever. "Don't hang up for a minute, please? Please, just talk. Talk about anything, but don't hang up. I — I get scared. Scared you won't like me, I —"

Rick's door opened and his father looked in. "You studying, Rick?" he asked.

Guiltily, Rick covered the phone receiver. "I was just — talking to somebody."

"Mmmm." David frowned. "Better get to it." He folded his arms, waiting for Rick to hang up.

"Listen," Rick said, trying to make her understand without — his father was frowning. "I'll call you later, I gotta get off." He lowered his voice, blocking his face with his hand. "My *dad's* here. . . ."

He went to the hospital extra early the next morning to make up for maybe not studying enough. He drove his Yamaha to the back parking lot, a camera with his new, extra-sharp zoom lens around his neck. If he took some pictures of actual tissue samples today, he could compare them to the ones presented in his books. He might not *learn* anything, but the challenge of the camera angles appealed to him.

He locked the motorbike to the fence, then jogged over to the hospital's back entrance. Glancing to his right, he noticed a doctor dressed in surgical scrubs and a woman standing by a car. The man resembled his father and he squinted, trying to see better. He still couldn't tell, so he lifted his camera, peering through the lens and zooming in to sharp focus.

It *was* his father. And the woman Rick had seen running out of his office the day before. She was upset for some reason, crying, and Rick automatically clicked the camera shutter.

Her hand, fumbling inside her pocketbook, coming out with a cigarette. *Click.* His father lighting it. His hand grazing her hair. Her cheek.

The woman climbing into the car. The license plates. Clicking once. Twice. The car pulling away, his father standing there, watching.

Slowly, Rick lowered the camera, afraid to check his father's expression. Afraid to find out.

Chapter 5

Rick didn't go to the hospital the next day, but stayed in his darkroom, developing the pictures while Lonnie watched. They were dry, finally, and he turned on the light, studying them. On photographic paper, it looked worse. Black and white in more ways than one.

Lonnie picked up a picture of the woman. "She looks sad. Maybe she has a brain tumor or something."

Rick didn't answer, carrying a sheaf of pictures to his desk.

Lonnie followed him. "Do you think she's trying to blackmail him? People are always doing that."

Rick sat down, sifting through photographs, frowning. "I don't know." He stood up, stuffing one photograph under his arm. "Come on, let's go."

"Where?"

"Just come on," he said, taking her hand.

They hurried downstairs, past the living room where Rick's mother was practicing the Brahms concerto.

"See ya, Mom," Rick said, without pausing.

Tina glanced up. "Wait, where are you going?" She came out after them. "Rick? Why don't you go with Philip and his friends down to the tennis club?"

But the front door had already closed after them.

That afternoon, Rick sat in front of the computer at his father's office, going through names. The door opened, and May came in with some files.

"Oh." She paused. "Are you working today?"

"No," he said quickly. "I'm just — looking for a name."

She tilted her head, confused. "Of a patient? What name?"

Rick turned off the power and the green light slowly disappeared from the screen. "It's okay. It isn't here. . . ." He pushed away from the terminal and hurried to the door.

"Rick?" May called after him. "Rick, is everything okay?"

Lonnie was waiting outside, near the elevators.

"Was it there?" she asked.

"No." He took her arm. "Come on."

"Where?"

"Just come on," he said.

He stopped the motor scooter in front of a large Spanish-style house, resting his foot on the curb to keep the bike upright.

"Why are we here?" Lonnie asked, sitting behind him, her arms around his waist.

"This is her address," Rick said grimly. "Bobby's brother works for the DMV — I gave him her license number."

"She's not a patient? You're sure?"

"I checked through everything." He climbed off the bike, put his hand out to help Lonnie off, then dragged the bike up onto the sidewalk.

"So, now what do we do?" Lonnie asked uneasily.

Rick wheeled the bike over to a tree in the park across from the house, letting it fall on the grass beside it. "We're going to wait here for a while."

"Rick." Reluctantly, Lonnie followed him. "Maybe it's none of our business. Maybe — maybe we should just forget it."

He shook his head. "I can't. There was something — weird. I mean, who is she? Why wouldn't he tell me when I asked?"

Lonnie shrugged, looking at the grass so he wouldn't have to see the obvious, unhappy answer in her expression. He sat down with his back against the tree, folding his arms and, resigned, Lonnie lowered herself to the ground next to him.

It was dusk and they were still in the park. Lonnie had fallen asleep, her head pillowed on his knee, and except for resting his hand on her hair, Rick hadn't moved, his eyes fixed on the house. Waiting.

Chapter 6

School was starting soon and Lois insisted on Tina bringing Sarah to the factory to pick out some new shirts. She moved along the shelves, taking a shirt here, another there, loading them into Sarah's eager arms. Tina trailed behind them, laughing.

"Oh, and this one," Lois said, selecting a light blue French-cut, "and," she pulled out a peach-colored shirt, "this one, and —"

"Enough!" Tina said, amused. "That's more than she can wear."

Lois held up a pink French-cut T-shirt. "What about this one?"

"Yeah!" Sarah said.

Lois dropped it on top of the pile. "It's fun to give them to someone who *appreciates* them. Lonnie hates everything I like. My clothes —"

Tina laughed. "And you hate *her* clothes."

"What clothes?" Lois asked, so theatrically that several workers glanced up. "She doesn't want *clothes*. An old battered pair of jeans, the more holes the better. School starts next week and she hasn't got anything to wear!" She held the door leading to the parking lot and Sarah struggled out with her new shirts.

"Come and have lunch with us," Tina suggested.

Lois shook her hair, tucking some loose hair underneath her bandanna. "Can't — I'm swamped."

"You and Harvey need a vacation."

"What would we do on a vacation?" Lois said. "We'd go *nuts* together."

"Lonnie can stay with us!" Sarah said, very enthusiastic.

"Sure," Tina said, less so. She glanced at Lois. "Sarah.... Go wait in the car a minute. I want to talk to Lois."

"I won't listen," Sarah promised.

Tina smiled. "Scram!"

Sarah shrugged, carrying her new shirts over to the car.

"So," Lois said, somewhat stiff.

Tina glanced at the car. "Rick and Lonnie have been spending a lot of time together...."

"Rick's the only person Lonnie likes to be with." Lois grinned wryly. "I'm not kidding."

Tina didn't smile back. "They're very young. I don't want them to get involved."

Lois put an arm around her, walking her to the car. "You're overreacting."

"Maybe...."

44

"Lonnie needs a friend." Lois paused. "So does Rick."

"I know. It just worries me because of —" Tina stopped.

"Lonnie's changed," Lois said quickly, "believe me. Besides, if there was something physical going on, I'd know it." She tightened her arm on Tina's shoulders before removing it. "Let them enjoy it. They're good for each other."

Tina nodded, but her expression was unconvinced.

It was the day before school started and, with Lonnie sitting behind him, Rick cruised past the woman's house. There was a car parked in front and he slowed the motorbike.

"Not again," Lonnie groaned. "This is like a stakeout — it's all we do anymore. We've never even *seen* her. Not once!"

Rick brought the bike closer, until he could see the license plate. He smiled. "She's home!"

They sat, as usual, in the park. Lonnie, long since resigned to the situation, had brought along some sandwiches.

"Here." She handed one to Rick. "I've got one turkey, and one just cheese." She handed him the turkey. "My mother keeps asking me where I've been. I make up all these places. The old mission. State Street. The beach. Today I'm supposed to be at my shrink's —" She sat up straighter, seeing movement across the street. "Rick."

He stared for a few seconds, then slowly brought up his camera, gritting his teeth as he focused on his father and the woman kissing. He took one picture, then another as the kiss grew more passionate. He stared through the viewfinder for one last second, then let the camera fall around his neck.

"Rick," Lonnie said hesitantly.

He didn't answer, hurrying off through the trees, his fists clenched.

"Rick, wait!" Lonnie ran after him, grabbing his arm. "Put it out of your mind, don't think about —"

"Oh, yeah?" He spun around to face her. "Well, what — what am I supposed to think about when —" He stopped, his voice shaking. "When my mother, when she —" He stopped again, fists tightening. "He always told us about love, and honor, and —" Suddenly very close to tears, he pulled her over in a fierce hug. "We're not like them," he said, his face pressed against her neck. "We're not like anybody else! We'll never hurt each other, or leave each other, or — or be unfaithful!" Crying now, he held her tightly against him.

He didn't go home for a long time, not until well after dark. His mother was in the living room with a couple of students, but he didn't pause on his way to the stairs.

"Ricky?" his mother called cheerfully. "Is that you?"

He hurried upstairs without answering, running into Philip in the hall.

"Get out of my way," Rick said, impatient.

"What?" Philip grinned and pushed him off-balance. "*You* get out of the way."

Rick scowled and shoved past him.

"Bobby called," Philip said uncertainly. "He wants to know if you and me can play —"

"I don't want to!"

Sarah, wearing a light pink summer nightgown, came to her bedroom door. "I know where you've been," she said in a sing-song voice. "With L-O-N-N-I-E. . . ."

He strode past her to his bedroom, slamming the door. Without bothering to turn on the light, he threw himself onto the bed, resting his head on folded arms.

There was a knock on the door. "Rick?" his mother asked.

He pulled a pillow over his head.

"There's some chicken casserole in the oven for you," she said through the door. "We waited and waited —"

"I'm not hungry."

"I just wish you'd call me." Tina paused. "When you're going to be late, I mean. I cook a nice meal, we all wait for you — I thought you'd be home early." She turned the knob, finding that the door was locked. "Rick? Hey. You're locking the door now?"

He sighed and pushed away from the bed, crossing to the door and slowly opening it.

She smiled at him. "Thanks a *lot*." She stopped smiling, worried by the slump to his shoulders. "What's the matter?"

He shook his head, too tired and upset to say anything.

"What is it?" she asked.

He was going to say "nothing," but found himself hugging her instead, fresh tears hurting against his eyes. "I love you, Mom."

"I love you, too." She leaned back to look at his face. "Are you okay?"

He couldn't tell her, there was no way that he could tell her. "I'm" — he managed a smile — "fine."

She studied him, not quite convinced, but nodded. "Don't worry about that exam — you'll do great."

His smile weakened.

"You should have the worries these Nigerian boys have," she said, trying to cheer him up. "All their funds have been cut off from home — they're stranded. I'm trying to find them some part-time —" She stopped, seeing that he wasn't listening. "Rick? They're —" She indicated the stairs.

He nodded, stuffing his hands into his pockets.

"Look," Tina said, "I know you're trying to help Lonnie because I asked you to — it's sweet. But you've got to look out for yourself, too." She patted his face and went downstairs.

Sarah came out of her room, poised to run

in case he yelled at her. "You — wanna play Atari?"

He shook his head. "Not now."

"Nobody will ever play with me," she said, sulking.

"So, ask Dad." He smiled slightly. "Why don't you ask your dad?"

"He's not home."

"Oh. An emergency?" Rick asked sarcastically. "A meeting? He had to — work late?" He shook his head, the smile bitter now, and went into his room, closing the door. Relocking it.

Chapter 7

At breakfast the next morning, Rick couldn't eat. Sarah and Philip were all excited about school starting, discussing it in loud voices, gesturing with cereal spoons between mouthfuls. Tina was nodding and responding, but kept glancing at Rick, obviously worried.

"You wait," Philip was saying. "This year, me and Artie're going to kick a —"

"Philip," Tina said, frowning.

"I didn't mean —"

"I know what you meant." She reached over to touch Rick's arm. "Are you okay? Would you like me to make you some scrambled eggs maybe?"

"Yeah," Philip said. "Eggs'd be —"

"No, no, pancakes," Sarah interrupted. "Mom, can we have pancakes?"

"Good morning." David came in, fixing his tie, bending over Tina's shoulder to give her a peck on the cheek.

Rick looked away, his hands tightening into fists under the table.

David straightened up. "You shoulda *seen* your dad last night. I was in rare form. *Moi*," he did a mock bow, "got a standing '*O*.' " He sat down, reaching for the orange juice. "I got up in front of all those dried up doctors, tore the hospital apart, and put it back together again in about two minutes. They ate it up. Wanted more. . . ." He glanced around the table for their reactions. "So. You guys ready to start school this morning? I guess I don't need to tell you what I expect from all of you this year."

Rick pushed away from the table, heading for the stairs.

"Rick," Tina said, "please try to eat something."

"You have an upset stomach?" his father asked.

"I'm *okay*!" He ran upstairs before his father could pull him back.

He was in the bathroom, washing his face, when David appeared in the doorway.

"What's the matter, pal?" he asked.

Rick pulled a towel off the rack, pressing it against his face.

"You nervous about the science test?"

"No," Rick said through the towel.

"You've been goofing off for weeks," David said. "It's catching up with you."

Rick lowered the towel, looking at him. His father. Someone he'd always been able to talk to. And if he couldn't talk to his father, he could talk to his mother. Only now — lately — looking at his father, standing there all concerned and sympathetic, like he was the Perfect Father or something, when it wasn't *true* — Rick focused down on the towel, twisting it in his hands.

"Look," David said, "these tests may be a stupid way to evaluate a person's capacity, but you know the rules, so you can't argue the call." He leaned forward, giving Rick a playful shake. "Just give it everything you've got. Wow 'em! Make me proud." He paused "Existentialism?"

"I don't know," Rick said. "I don't *care*."

His father studied him, nodded shortly, and turned to go.

This was his *father*. Someone he'd always respected, admired, *loved*. Someone who always put his family first and would never, *never* — there had to be an explanation, a reason, a — "Dad?"

His father turned and they looked at each other, Rick so eager for an explanation, something that would make it all okay again, that he could feel himself straining forward.

"Better make it quick," David said, breaking the silence. "I have to hurry."

Rick slumped back, the hope gone as fast as it had come. "Nothing," he muttered, and his father left the room.

A couple of minutes later, in his bedroom, Rick heard the BMW start up and he moved to the window. As his father backed out of the driveway, his mother ran out with his gym bag.

"Honey?" she called.

He stopped the car.

"You forgot this," she said, handing it through the window.

"I think I'm getting senile," David said, dropping the bag on the backseat, then bringing his hand back to the gearshift.

"You also forgot to kiss me."

"Now I *know* I'm getting senile." He leaned out the window to kiss her and, watching, Rick felt a sharp pain starting in his stomach.

The kiss was over now and his mother was on her way back to the house.

"Looking good there," David said, then grinned. "Looking *real* good."

Rick stepped away from the window, so angry that it was a struggle to keep from slamming his fist into the wall. Who the hell was his father trying to kid?

Breakfast was even worse at Lonnie's house. She sat at the table, too nervous to eat, while her mother yelled at her, and her father concentrated on the newspaper.

"I'm furious!" Lois said, hands on her hips. "You had an appointment with the psychiatrist yesterday at three. You didn't show, you didn't call me, you didn't call *him* —"

Lonnie shrugged. "It's a waste of time. He hates me anyway."

"That's what you always say! How many doctors have we gone through?"

"It's boring!" Lonnie yelled back. " 'Okay,

Lonnie,'" she said, imitating her doctor, "'how are things?'" She pretended to look at a wristwatch.

"Your father and I pay a lot of money —"

"I didn't ask you to!"

Her mother ignored that. "Would you mind telling me what you've been *doing* every afternoon?"

"Reading," Lonnie said, not meeting her eyes. "Nothing. . . ."

Lois let out an irritated breath, then scowled at her husband. "That's right, Harvey — just sit there! Don't get involved!"

Harvey dropped the paper. "I'm involved!" he said defensively. "I'm listening."

"Right," Lois said. "It seems like I'm the only one around here who's *concerned*."

"Mom, it was only one time —" Lonnie started.

"One time? Are you kidding me? This has been going on for years!" Lois' hands fluttered through her hair. "You tell me you're at school — then they call and say you're not. You tell me you're at a friend's — and I call and they hardly know you. You never tell me the truth! It's always the same! I try and try, and you never like anything!" She stopped pacing. "This is the deal," she said. "You skip classes this year, and I'm sending you off to boarding school." She strode out of the room.

Lonnie looked at her father, who quickly buried himself in the newspaper.

"Please, Daddy?" Lonnie asked, her voice shaking. "Please be on my side?"

The high school lawn was crowded, no one wanting to leave the sunshine and start another long year. Lonnie clung to Rick's arm as they walked toward the main entrance. Other students, noticing her, exchanged glances or whispered remarks. Each time someone passed, Lonnie clutched Rick's arm more tightly.

"I have to do good this year," she said, "or I have to go away to boarding school." She stopped walking, panic setting in as they approached the main doors. "Rick, what if — I'm scared I'll never —"

"It's going to be all right," he said, putting a protective arm around her waist.

"Hey, Rick!" Bobby yelled, trotting over.

"Uh, hi." Rick didn't look at him. "What's up?"

"Hi, Lonnie," Bobby said.

Lonnie nodded quickly. Nervously.

"We're going over to the arcade after registration," Bobby said. "You guys feel like coming?"

Rick moved closer to Lonnie, feeling her tense. "Maybe."

"Well," Bobby nodded uncertainly, "try." He trotted back over to Jeb and a girl from their class, Sherry.

"You're getting real stuck up, Rick," the girl said. "You know that?"

He didn't answer, steering Lonnie inside.

"It's hard," she whispered, hesitating near the door. "Walking in here. Everyone knows what I tried to do — they all look at me."

"You're with me," Rick said, his arm moving up around her shoulders. "No one's going to bother you." He guided her through the hall, his walk defiant.

Alone, it was awful. Because they were in different classes, they had to register separately, and Lonnie was scared. She stood at the back of the registration line, hunched over her books, afraid to look at anyone or anything. Everyone looked at *her*, but no one approached, and she hunched more, feeling very, very alone.

They went to the arcade after school, Lonnie selecting a game in a far-off corner, punching at the control buttons. It was very noisy, everyone laughing and rowdy, rock videos flashing on a screen on one wall, a large group gathered around watching.

"I hated it!" Lonnie slammed at the buttons, knocking off targets in bright explosions of color. "I'm never going back! Never!"

"It'll get easier," Rick said, right behind her. "Really."

Three boys cruising around from one machine to another wandered over.

"Hey, Rick," one of them said cheerfully. "You playing soccer this year?"

Lonnie looked up, flushing deeply as she recognized them. Seeing her, the boys looked just as uncomfortable, and a tense minute passed before Lonnie ran toward the exit.

"Hey, Lonnie!" Rick went after her. "Lonnie, wait!" By the time he caught up to her, they were in the parking lot. "What's the matter?" he asked, out of breath.

She spun away from him. "I don't want to talk about it!"

"What happened in there?"

"What is this?" she demanded. "The third degree? Will you stop it? Just — stop!"

"Did those guys do something to you?" he asked, confused.

"It's none of your business!"

He yanked her back as she started away. "I want you to tell me!"

"I couldn't —" She struggled to get away. "*I couldn't help it!*" She twisted free, everyone staring as she ran past.

Rick ran after her, grabbing her arm and jerking her to a stop. "Help *what*?"

"I —" She realized people were staring and flushed more. "I couldn't help it, I couldn't! I —" She shuddered suddenly, arms wrapping around herself. "I wanted somebody to like me!"

"Y-you —" Rick stopped, understanding what she meant. "You mean, one of those guys?" He went on when she didn't answer. "Which one? I want to know which one."

"Don't ask me that, Rick. *Please* don't ask —"

"Was it Darryl?! Do you mean Darryl?!"

"I —" Lonnie shook her head, trembling.

"I don't know. The names. . . ."

Rick grabbed her hand, pulling her back toward the arcade, both furious and jealous. "Point him out to me," he said grimly.

"It wasn't just one!" Lonnie said, and burst into tears. "It wasn't just one, Rick."

Rick stopped, staring at her. He dropped her hand, moving away as she crumpled over, looking as though she were trying to hold herself together with her arms.

"I want to go home," she said quietly.

Rick looked at her, then strode toward the arcade, his fists tight.

"Rick, no!" Lonnie shouted after him. "Don't! Please? Don't!"

He yanked the door open.

"If you go in there, I'll — I'll never speak to you again! I won't." She turned and ran away, almost crashing into Bobby, Jeb, and Sherry. She stared at them, embarrassed and crying, then started running again, out of the parking lot and down the street.

"What a *psycho*," Sherry said, staring after her.

Rick stormed into the arcade, shoving past and through people, looking for the boys. He saw them hanging around one of the machines and grabbed the one closest to him, slamming him against the wall, then punching with both fists. The other two boys jumped on him, swinging, and Rick swung back, trying to fight all of them at once, trying to get back at them, trying to *kill* them. . . .

58

Chapter 8

When he got home, he refused to tell his parents anything, going straight to his room. His mother hovered around, bringing trays of food, and his father kept trying to examine him. Finally, so his mother wouldn't worry, he admitted that he had been in a fight and would they *please* leave him alone. They agreed, but his father insisted on taking him to the hospital the next morning for a check-up with their family doctor, Dr. Madsen.

"Okay," Dr. Madsen said in the X-ray room. "I just want a few pictures of those ribs. You doing okay?"

Rick moved to the spot the technician indicated. His face hurt, the bruises puffy and swollen, and Dr. Madsen had already put a couple of stitches in the cut over his eye.

"Okay," Dr. Madsen said, patting him on the shoulder. "I'll be out in the hall. We'll have you out of here in no time, Rick."

David, pacing in the hallway, stopped when Dr. Madsen came out. "Well?"

"He's tender around the ribs, so we're raying it. He's got a nonsurgical belly, no internal injuries." Dr. Madsen glanced over. "He's taken quite a beating."

David nodded glumly. "As long as he's here, you'd better run a blood for drugs. Check him for alcohol, too." He shook his head. "He's been acting so strange lately."

"Well, we'll give him a complete physical. He's overdue."

"Yeah." David sighed. "I don't know what's going on with him anymore."

"You try to talk to him?"

"He *won't* talk," David said, frustrated. He took a sip of his almost cold coffee. "All I can get out of him is that he was in a fight."

"It's very difficult these days, to be a teenager."

David shook his head. "Rick's — different. He's not some goofball."

The X-ray room door opened and Rick came out, both his walk and his expression stiff.

"Okay, Rick," Dr. Madsen said cheerfully, ushering him back to the examination room. "Just come on in here and I'll check you over."

Following them, David glanced at his watch. "You've got the science exam at two. Maybe I should call and arrange for another day."

Rick scowled. "I told you. I'm taking it."

"Well, it's ridiculous. You have to be in tip-top shape. I want you to do *well*."

"I feel great!" Rick said sarcastically, then mimicked his father's inflections. "Ready to show the world, give it all my heart and soul." His smile was closer to a sneer. "How's that?"

David looked stunned. "Rick, what *is* this?"

"Don't worry, Dad. You're gonna be proud of me." His laugh was vicious. "Don't you worry."

"Here." Dr. Madsen moved in between them, putting his hand on David's shoulder. "You go on, and we'll finish up."

Rick gave his father a cold look, then went into the examining room.

David released a hard, irritated breath. "See what I mean?"

"I'll talk to him," Dr. Madsen said. He walked into the examining room, closing the door behind him. "So," he said, washing his hands, "you feel like talking, Rick?"

Rick shrugged and Dr. Madsen crossed to the table, gently probing the bruises on his face, checking the suture.

"This over a girl?" he asked.

Rick shook his head.

"You know," Dr. Madsen moved his hands down, going over Rick's ribs again, "it only makes it more difficult, keeping it all inside. Get it out." He prodded Rick's stomach at the tender spots. "Talk to your dad, he's a good guy. Get some lines of communication open."

Rick didn't answer, stiffening, but not because of pain in his stomach.

Dr. Madsen looked at him for a long minute. "It's hard to be a parent. We want what's best for our kids, but somehow, it doesn't always seem that way. . . ." He paused, waiting for a reaction, not getting one. "Talk to your dad, Rick. Tell him what's on your mind, what's going on. I promise you that once you get it off your chest, it won't seem so insurmountable."

Rick didn't move or speak; he stared at the eye chart across the room, waiting silently for this to be over.

Tina, outside gardening, turned as a car pulled into the driveway. It was Bobby, climbing out of his old Cadillac.

She waved across the yard at him. "Rick's not here."

"Is he okay?" Bobby asked. "We got him out of there as fast as we could. . . ."

Tina nodded. "David took him down to Dr. Madsen's this morning. He's over at the school now, taking that test for the science program."

Bobby nodded, hands in his pockets, shifting his weight from one foot to the other.

Tina put down her trowel. "Something wrong?"

"Well —" Bobby shifted some more. "Rick hardly speaks to me anymore. I just wondered if you knew . . . why."

Tina sighed. "You heard of the terrible twos? Well, Rick's in the terrible teens." She smiled wryly. "He's distant and cold and disgusted with *everybody*."

"Well — maybe," Bobby said. "But —"

"Really," Tina said. "Don't take it personally."

Rick sat in the examination room, alone except for the supervisor, who was correcting papers at her desk. The exam was a thick sheaf of multiple choice questions and, a pencil clenched in his hands, Rick went through the pages, crossing off answers without even reading the questions. Finished, he dropped the pencil and carried the test up to the front of the room.

The supervisor looked up, startled, and he handed her the pages.

"You *can't* be finished," she said, glancing at the clock, then at the exam. "It's impossible."

He was already gone.

He drove the Yamaha to Lonnie's house, driving as fast as it would go, swerving around corners and in and out of traffic. He sped through stop signs and over potholes, his tape deck blasting *The Magic Flute*.

At Lonnie's house, he let the bike drop onto the sidewalk and ran to the front door, falling against the doorbell. When she opened the door, he stumbled into her arms, hugging her tightly.

"Oh, Rick!" she gasped. "Your poor face!"

"I just wanna be with you," he said weakly, his face pressed into her hair. "I *have* to be with you."

"Oh, Rick." She pulled him inside and they stood in the hall, embracing.

"I felt so dirty," she whispered. "All those boys, staring." She pressed closer. "I never want to go in that place again, never."

"Just put your arms around me," he said. "Hold me. . . ."

They clung to each other, Rick planting frantic kisses, Lonnie's kisses more soothing.

"Your poor face," she said softly, holding his cheeks.

"I just want to get in bed with you," he said. "And pull the covers over my head, and hold you close . . . and never wake up."

She pulled him into a hug. "Don't hate me, Rick," she begged. "Please don't hate me."

"I could *never* hate you. You're the first girl I've ever — and you're the only one I ever *want* to be with. Do you understand that?" He hesitated. "I — love you."

She stared at him, her eyes huge.

"Please, hold me," he said. "Please?"

She kissed him and they clung tightly to each other.

"Let's go upstairs," she whispered.

They were in the bed for a long time, Rick hanging on desperately, Lonnie stroking his shoulders and back, her hands gentle and loving.

"I don't ever want to get up," he said. "I don't want to go back to school. I don't want to brush my teeth, or eat, or drink — I don't even want to *breathe*."

Home from work, Lois let her shoulder bag fall onto the kitchen table.

"Alma?" she called.

There was no answer and she moved to the hallway.

"Alma?"

"What is it?" Harvey asked, coming in behind her.

"Alma doesn't seem to be here," Lois said, annoyed. "She's supposed to stay until five. . . . I have a feeling she never does." Hearing loud music coming from Lonnie's room, Lois went upstairs to ask her.

Lonnie's door was closed and Lois opened it, knocking as she did.

"Lonnie?" she asked. "Where's Alma —" She stared, seeing them in bed.

Rick and Lonnie looked up, startled, and Lonnie yanked the sheet up to cover herself.

Lois stared at them, then stepped into the hall, slamming the door shut.

"Lois?" Harvey asked, halfway up the stairs. "What's the matter? What is it?"

Lonnie hurried out of the room, pulling on a bathrobe. "It's not the way you think!" she said. "We weren't —"

Harvey looked at Lois, at his daughter, then shoved past her into the bedroom. Rick, zipping his jeans and halfway into his shirt, spun around defensively. Harvey stopped, stunned.

"Oh, Rick," he said. "Oh, hell."

They stared at each other, Rick stricken.

"Get out of here," Harvey said. "Just get out."

Rick just stood there and Harvey lunged at him, shaking him by the shoulders.

"You get out of this house!" he yelled. "And never come back! You hear me?!"

Rick didn't resist as Harvey pushed him out into the hall.

Lonnie rushed over to defend him. "Daddy, no! Don't!"

Harvey didn't pause, gripping Rick's shoulder and shoving him toward the stairs. "Stay out of this, Lonnie!" He glanced back at her, furious. "And put your clothes on! You don't have to show everything you've got!"

Lonnie stayed in the hall for a second, then something exploded inside and she stormed into her room. She kicked a chair over, then knocked everything off her white dresser before yanking the drawers out and spilling the clothes out onto the floor.

"It isn't dirty!" she screamed. "It isn't like with those other boys!" She stared into the mirror, trembling uncontrollably. "I wish I was dead." She saw Lois' reflection in the doorway. "Do you hear me, Mother? *I wish I was dead*!"

Chapter 9

When David got home, dulled from over five hours of surgery, he was depressed and exhausted. Sarah ran to meet him in the upstairs hallway.

"Daddy!" she said. "Guess what I saw on television? This guy said the planet was dying —"

He gave her a half-hearted hug. "I'm tired, honey."

"Yeah, but, I mean it! See, we're cutting down all the trees, and polluting the air, and —"

"Honey," David sighed, "we'll talk about it later. I'm completely bushed." He continued past her and downstairs.

"Well, okay," she said. "But this man said we're in a cosmic tailspin." Her father was long gone. "Whatever that means."

In his room, Rick was standing in front of his bookcase. Not that he felt like reading. He pulled a book — one of his least favorite books — out, and opened it, taking out the photographs he had hidden inside.

David and the Woman kissing in front of her house. David and the Woman in the hospital parking lot.

"Rick?" Sarah asked from the door.

He flinched, quickly hiding the pictures behind his back. Sarah came into the room, looking around at the books and papers on the desk, and the clothes lying over one chair and on the floor by the closet. Rick's room was generally Army-barrack neat.

"The world's in a mess, huh?" she said.

Rick didn't smile.

"You know what I saw on TV?" she asked, going on when he didn't say anything. "They're cutting down a million trees every day in the Amazon. It's gonna change the climate *all over the world*." She looked up at him unhappily. "Maybe that's why all those whales keep beaching themselves, you think? Like an epidemic. You know — suicide."

"Maybe so," Rick said quietly.

"Can I borrow your book on whales?"

He reached onto his shelves, pulling it out. "Take it."

"I'll be careful," she promised.

He nodded, then found himself grabbing more books, piling them into her arms.

"Take what you want," he said. "I don't want them anymore. . . ." He slammed over to his desk, yanking the photographs out of his back pocket and dumping them into a drawer which he slammed shut. Then he just sat there, elbows on the desk, resting his face on his fists.

Sarah stared at her big brother, eyes wide and frightened, then hurried out of the room.

Rick pressed his face into his fists, not caring that his bruises hurt. Not really caring about *anything*.

"Uh, Rick?" Now *Philip* was in the doorway. "You okay?"

He didn't answer, hunching over his desk.

"Uh, sorry," Philip said uncertainly, and left.

Lonnie huddled under her blankets, alone except for her kitten, clutching him to her chest. There was a quiet knock on the door and her father came in.

"Lonnie?" he asked.

Lonnie crumpled over even more.

Harvey came over, sitting awkwardly on the edge of the bed. He cleared his throat. "Uh, Lonnie. . . ." He stopped, twisting his hands uneasily in his lap, not sure how he felt, or what to say, or — he coughed, anger, embarrassment, and disappointment all churning around somewhere inside.

Finally, Lonnie broke the silence. "You're going to send me away now, right?"

"I'd like for you to go to your mother and apologize," Harvey said.

"It's not like it'll *help*," Lonnie said, very bitter.

"She's" — Harvey searched for the right word, but couldn't find it — "upset."

"I can't be what she wants me to be, Daddy. I just can't."

More silence.

Awkwardly, Harvey stood up. "You'd better get your room straightened up now."

"Daddy?"

He paused on his way to the door.

"See," Lonnie struggled to a sitting position. "Rick is the only person that likes me just the way I am. Do you know what I mean? I mean — he likes everything about me, *everything*! He —" She gulped. "I love him, Daddy. He's all I can think about. When I close my eyes even. I see his face in my mind and I want to be *with* him."

"Oh, honey." Harvey patted her hair with a clumsy hand. "You're — a little girl, Lonnie. You're gonna feel this way — a dozen times before you're seventeen. You know what it's called? Puppy love." He gave her hair one last nervous pat and then left the room.

As the door closed, Lonnie slumped back onto her pillow, picking up her kitten and holding him very close.

It was very late. Harvey sat at the kitchen table, nursing a scotch, while Lois paced back and forth on the linoleum, more than one drink ahead of him.

"I know you," she said, pointing an accusing finger. "You want to give her a free ticket to do *anything* she wants in this house."

Harvey sighed. "That isn't true, Lois. I'm as upset as you are!"

"Then why don't you ever do anything?" she wanted to know, hands on her hips. "Why don't you ever take part?"

"I sent the kid home, didn't I?" He paused. "We have to tell David and Tina."

"That's right," Lois said, very sarcastic. " 'David and Tina.' That's all you care about!"

He sighed again, pouring more scotch into his glass. "Will you leave me alone?"

She started for the hall.

"Where are you going?"

"I want to make sure she's still in her bed!" Lois headed for the stairs.

Harvey leaned back in his chair, taking a long swallow of his drink. He looked at the clock above the stove. Three A.M.

"Harvey!" Lois shouted. "Come here!"

"What?" He jumped up. "What is it?"

"She's gone!"

"Are you sure?" David asked into the telephone a few minutes later, then covered the phone with his hand. "Rick's here, isn't he?"

"Of course," Tina said, but swung out of bed anyway, pulling on her bathrobe.

David went to check, knocking lightly on the door before pushing it open. "Rick?" He turned on the light, seeing the bed empty and still neatly made. "He's not here!"

Tina rushed into the room, seeing both the

empty bed and the comparative disarray. "It's not Rick," she said, "it's Lonnie! *She's* the one —"

David stiffened. "My car." He ran past her to the stairs. "My keys were in my car."

"He wouldn't do that," Tina said, following him. "He wouldn't take your car!"

Rick smiled as he guided the BMW along the highway, speeding in the early morning light. Lonnie sat next to him, also smiling, reaching forward to turn up the radio that was blaring new wave music.

"What do we do for money?" she asked, giggling.

He brushed a kiss across her hair, tightening his arm around her shoulders. "I've got a little — we'll go as far as we can!" He looked back at the road. "We'll ditch the car in Vegas."

"We'll go someplace where nobody knows us, huh?"

Rick laughed. "Where nobody can even *find* us."

"We'll get jobs," Lonnie said. "Find our own place. . . ."

Rick leaned his head against hers. "Listen to music, stay up all night, watch the sunrise. . . ."

A police siren wailed behind them and they both stiffened, Lonnie turning to look over her shoulder.

"Don't!" Rick said. "Don't look back!"

"They've got their light on!"

Rick pressed down on the gas, the police car careening after them. They couldn't get caught — they *couldn't*! If they did, their parents would — he saw an access road and swerved onto it, trying to lose the squad car. But another police car came around the bend, heading right at them, and Rick jumped on the brakes with both feet. Both cars skidded, Rick trying to control the BMW, the smell of burning rubber hot and strong in the car. The car screeched to a neck-jarring stop, police officers jumping out and surrounding them. Caught.

Chapter 10

The police station was in a small town at the edge of the desert. It was hot and dusty, and the wind was blowing sand everywhere. The police took them to an interrogation room, empty except for three folding chairs, a card table, and a barred window.

Rick stood at the window, staring out, each hand gripping a bar. Lonnie sat in one of the chairs, slumped forward on the table, her head on her arms. An officer stood guarding the doorway.

"You think you've got it bad at home?" the cop asked, large arms folded across his chest. "Try running away again, and we'll let you spend some time at a juvenile detention center. See how you like it *there*." He shook his head. "Stealing a car. . . . *Next* time, your parents won't be so willing to come and bail you out."

Lonnie looked up. "Will they be here soon?"

The police officer shrugged.

Harvey drove across the desert, David in the passenger's seat next to him. David stared out through the windshield, his face set, and Harvey kept glancing over, uneasy.

"David?" he asked. "Remember that time we took your old man's car? It was no big deal — maybe this isn't either. Maybe we're all getting carried away."

"They were running away," David said grimly. "It wasn't some joy ride. Wake up and smell the fire." His hands tightened. "Rick's never been in trouble before. Never. It's just since Lonnie got back."

"Are you saying it's all Lonnie's fault?"

"Well, *Lonnie's* the one with the problems — *that's* no secret."

Harvey looked at him for a long minute, shaking his head. "You ever thought that maybe *Rick* has some problems, too?"

"Oh, yeah," David said. "Big problems." He laughed shortly. "You know what I found out today? He flunked his test for that science program. A kid with an I.Q. around 140. A kid who's always excelled in everything!"

"I know, I know," Harvey said. "I've heard all about him. Since the day he was *born*. The genius, the wonderboy, Superkid!" Harvey's laugh was just as unfriendly. "Rick and his music. Rick and his photography. Rick and his *amazing* grasp of mathematical concepts. Rick and his future as a doctor." He bounced his fist off the steering wheel. "Did it ever occur to you that maybe you drive him too hard? That maybe he's rebelling?"

They were at the police station now and Harvey pulled into the parking lot, turning off the ignition.

Neither man spoke.

"Well." David reached for the door handle. "There's no point in continuing this."

"Rick was in my house yesterday afternoon," Harvey said quietly. "In *bed* with *my* daughter. Did you know that?"

David turned. "What are you talking about?"

"You heard me." Harvey slammed angrily out of the car, and David jumped out the other side.

"Who do you think was responsible for *that*?" David demanded.

"Oh, Lonnie," Harvey said, heading for the station. "*Definitely* Lonnie."

"She's the one who's . . . been around!"

Harvey paused with his hand on the front door. "Don't worry," he said, his voice dripping sarcasm. "You don't have to worry about Lonnie 'corrupting' your son anymore. Lois found a school in Arizona."

"Oh, yeah?" David scowled back. "How soon does she leave?"

"Monday morning! Is that soon enough for you?" Harvey stormed into the station, David right behind him, both furious.

It didn't take long. A lecture or two, fines to be paid, papers to be signed. David stood at the counter, going through the last of the papers while Rick waited in a nearby chair, very stiff, slowly rocking back and forth.

Harvey and Lonnie started for the door, Lonnie flinching away when her father tried to touch her shoulder. David indicated for Rick to get up, which he did, and they walked toward the door, avoiding each other's eyes.

"You're really not gonna press charges?" the sheriff asked. "Teach these kids a lesson?"

"No," David said.

"You'd better watch them," the sheriff warned. "I seen it a thousand times. You don't crack down, and they go from bad to worse." He handed David the BMW keys. "Your car's around back."

David nodded. "Let's get out of here," he said through his teeth.

They left the station, the fathers and their children, nobody speaking.

Rick stood by his bedroom window, still rocking slightly, *The Magic Flute* playing on his stereo.

"Rick?" Philip asked, just beyond the threshold.

"I'm not hungry."

"Nobody's asking you to eat." Philip shifted his weight, then pushed up his sweatshirt sleeves. "You, uh, wanna go over to the gym and play some racquetball?"

"No."

"Whatsa matter?" Philip asked, putting on a big grin. "You trying to be a homeboy or something?"

Rick didn't answer.

"What," Philip said, "you're not talking to me?"

Rick nodded. "You got it."

Philip's smile faded, his expression hurt. "What did I do? Just *tell* me."

It wasn't Philip's fault. It was hard to figure out whose fault it *was*, but it definitely wasn't Philip's. "Nothing," Rick said gently. "It isn't you."

Still hesitant, Philip came into the room. "What's this music?"

"You wouldn't like it."

"No, I like it sort of." Philip's grin was back. "Kind of." He threw his arms out in his opera singer imitation. "Ohhhdddellii aroma! Ohhhllaaaammeesolo!" He danced over behind his brother, boxing playfully. "And it's a right." He threw several mock punches. "A left. A hard jab to the jaw."

Rick turned abruptly, going over to the bed and lying down.

Philip let his hands fall. "You ever gonna come downstairs? I mean, you can't spend your *life* up here. You gotta come down *sometimes*."

"Maybe I'll kill myself," Rick said.

"Hey, great!" Philip jumped at him with a pillow, swatting at his head. "That's a great idea. Makes a lotta sense. Like all those kids I heard about."

Rick sat up, knocking the pillow out of the way, then grabbing Philip hard around the arms. "Knock it off!"

Philip backed away, looking scared. "I was teasing!" He brushed himself off, his hands fluttering. "Wow, you're a *lot* of fun. Laugh a minute. . . ." He left, banging the door shut on his way out.

When Rick was sure his brother was gone, he picked up the phone next to his bed, dialing slowly. It rang a few times, then Lois answered.

"Hello?" she asked. "Hello there. . . . Hello?"

Slowly, Rick hung up.

Lois looked at the phone as the dial tone sounded, then hung up. There was a small notebook on the counter and she pulled it over. Lonnie's notebook.

She carried it into the living room — white walls, modular furniture — where Lonnie was sitting on the leather couch gently patting Timmy.

Lois held out the notebook. "Is this yours?"

"Oh — yeah." Lonnie took it. "It's some poems." Her hand curled around the spiral. "Did you read them?"

"I don't snoop, Lonnie," Lois said stiffly. "I've always *tried* to respect your privacy."

"But you can read 'em," Lonnie said. "If you want to. . . ." She looked at her mother, ready — almost eager — to hand it back, but Lois made no move. Lonnie sighed and let it fall onto the couch. "Mama," she said, "don't make me go."

"It's a wonderful school."

"But I'll just fail! I'm no *good* in school."

"This is an opportunity for you, Lonnie." Lois spoke as though she were reading from the school catalog. "To change things."

"Please? Don't make me go!"

"Lonnie. . . ." Lois sighed. "The psychiatrist thinks —"

"He doesn't *know* anything. I never tell him the truth."

"Wonderful!" Lois said. "A hundred dollars an hour down the drain."

"But I will from now on — I promise." She put Timmy down, her hands shaking. "Look, you're right. I'll change. I'll try hard! I'll go back to regular school, and I'll study — and I won't see Rick, either. I'm gonna be *so* good. . . ."

"You *always* promise," Lois said, unyielding.

"Mama," Lonnie blinked, tears starting in her eyes. "*Please.* . . . Maybe I could go to Ojai and stay with Grandma for a few weeks . . . and then come back?"

Lois shook her head, the decision made. "It's for the best, Lonnie. Honest."

Lonnie ran for the stairs. "You never care what I want! Neither one of you!"

Lois ran after her, grabbing her by the arm. "We *love* you!" she said. "You're our daughter!"

Lonnie struggled, trying to get away. "You didn't want me!"

"Lonnie —"

"You think I didn't know? I've known that

for *years*. I heard you one time, talking to Tina about how you *had* to get married!"

Lois' hand loosened on her arm. "Oh, honey." Her shoulders crumpled. "Honey, I didn't mean —"

Lonnie stayed on the attack. "I was eight years old, and I came in from the backyard, and I could hear you saying how you never wanted kids . . . but you got pregnant and had to get married."

"Maybe in the beginning," Lois admitted, hunched over. "But after I saw you . . . I *wanted* you."

"You didn't want me before I was born, and you didn't want me *after*!"

"That isn't true. This house," Lois gestured around them, "*all* of this — it's for you."

"What a laugh! You won't even let me *live* here!"

"We've tried," Lois said. "We've done *everything*. Dancing lessons, and tennis, and French, and —"

"To get rid of me!" Lonnie shouted. "To get me out of your hair!"

The phone rang and she jerked away from her mother, running to the kitchen to answer it.

"No!" Lois ran after her. "Lonnie, no! I'll answer it!"

Lonnie grabbed the phone. "Rick?"

Lois hit the button, cutting the connection.

"I hate you!" Lonnie screamed, throwing the receiver, then swinging furiously at her mother with both fists. "I just hate you!" She ran up the stairs toward her room.

Lois was right behind her. "You hit me! You don't *do* that! Do you hear me?" She stopped on the stairs, unable to go on. "You don't . . . hit me," she said weakly, sinking down onto the steps.

Harvey ran in from the patio, a glass in his hand. "What is it? What's going on?"

"Oh, my God, Harvey." Lois covered her face with her hands. "I've lost her. I've really lost her."

That afternoon, David made Rick come outside to be in the sunshine and to have a talk. Rick slumped down in a patio chair, trying to ignore the yelling and laughing from the pool as Philip, Sarah, and Artie splashed around. David was in the lawn chair next to his, wearing his swimming trunks and drinking a glass of iced tea.

"What I don't understand," David said calmly, "is why you blew the test — *deliberately*. The mistakes you make now are going to affect your whole life. The school you go to, your career as a doctor —"

Rick jumped up, knocking over his chair in the process. "You never listen to me! I'm not going to be a doctor!"

"I can accept that," David said, very calm. "All I really want is for you to grow up to be a good man, a good person. A man of honor. Loving, truthful —"

"Like *you*?" Rick asked and headed for the

garden — somewhere, anywhere, that he could get *away*.

"Rick." David came after him. "Can't you get it through your head? I'm on your side. I'm your father, but I'm also your friend."

Rick spun around. "I already have a friend! Lonnie! I want to see Lonnie! She's the only person I can talk to!"

"That's not true," David said. "You can talk to me."

"She's the only one I *want* to talk to! She's all I care about in the whole damned world!"

"Now, look!" David yelled back, the two standing face to face, almost on top of each other. "You're not going to throw everything away for a deeply disturbed sixteen-year-old dropout! She's been in and out of psychiatrists' offices since she was a little kid!" David paused, trying — somehow — to get through to him. "Rick, she tried to *kill* herself!"

"Oh." Rick didn't flinch. "What do you want me to do? Turn my back on her? Would that make you happy? Is that what a *good man* does? Well, I'm not like you!"

"I'm not going to let you see her," David said.

Rick grabbed his father by the arms, ready to punch him. "You can't stop me!"

David jerked away, furious. "I've *already* stopped you! She's leaving in the morning!"

"I know what you are!" Rick tried to hit him. "You're a cheat and a hypocrite! You hear that? *I know!*"

David slapped him, hard, across the face, and they stared at each other. Then, Rick turned and ran for the house.

The photographs were on his desk, and Rick looked at them, one by one, over and over. His father and the Woman. His father and the Woman. Again and again.

The rest of the family was in the den. He could hear the television blaring and their laughter as he carried the pictures downstairs, zipping his jacket with his free hand.

He walked into the living room, sitting down at the piano. His mother's piano. He opened the Brahms concerto, studying the notes, then slowly tucked the pictures inside, closing the folder and replacing it.

He walked out to the foyer, once again listening to the sounds of the television and his family laughing and joking. He bent down, patting their dog's head as he slept on the front hall rug.

"See ya around, Ralph." He straightened up, closing his eyes.

The house. The way it sounded, the wood settling and creaking slightly; the way it smelled, the fragrance of the most recent barbecue drifting in through the slightly ajar sliding glass doors.... His *home*.

Rick opened his eyes, looking around the hall, up the stairs, in the living room, toward the den. Then, he opened the front door and slipped out into the night.

Chapter 11

Lonnie tried to pack for school, crying and throwing the clothes into a suitcase. Timmy was curled up on the bed, watching her and purring, oblivious to her slamming around.

Rick, out on her balcony, tapped on her window.

Lonnie flinched, then saw who it was and scrambled across the bed to let him in.

"Rick, they're making me go away," she said frantically. "They took my phone so I couldn't talk to you. I couldn't *tell* you!"

He wrapped her in a fierce hug, kissing her face, her hair, her ears. Hard, urgent kisses.

"I have to leave in the morning," she said, pressed tightly against him.

"Let's go," he said.

"I hate them! They wouldn't listen. I was *screaming*, and they wouldn't listen!"

Rick grabbed her jacket from a chair, pulling it around her shoulders. "Come on, we'll climb down. Don't be afraid."

Lonnie nodded, shoving her pillows under the bedcovers to resemble a body.

"Let's go."

"Wait." She picked up her kitten from the foot of the bed, holding him inside her jacket. "I can't leave Timmy. . . ." She turned the light off and followed him out to the balcony.

Rick drove the scooter recklessly, speeding down a dirt road just outside of Santa Barbara, jouncing over and through potholes. They were near the highway now and he careened up onto the blacktop, Lonnie clinging to him with one hand, protecting Timmy with the other. The tape deck was turned up all the way, the Thompson Twins singing "Bouncing."

"Rick! Be careful!" Lonnie yelled.

He swerved across the road, barely missing a car coming from the opposite direction. He swerved more to avoid it, the horn blaring as it passed, and the bike almost crashed into the cement retaining wall at the side of the road. Lonnie screamed, burying her face in his back as he skidded to a stop.

"You're gonna *kill* us!" she yelled.

"What's the difference?" he yelled back. "What if I do?"

"I've got my kitten," she said, crying. "I don't want to hurt my kitten."

Rick kicked the bike into motion again, driving crazily, steering up an embankment, heading straight for a cliff. He stopped at the very edge, balancing the bike with his legs, staring out over the far away city lights. Lonnie slumped against his back, exhausted, then slowly took her kitten out of her jacket.

"Don't be frightened, Timmy," she whispered, stroking his head. "Don't be scared."

"Tell me about it," Rick said, his voice just as soft.

"About what?"

"About —" He swallowed. "The time you cut your wrists."

"Why do you want to hear *that*?"

"I just keep thinking." He rocked the bike, bringing it closer to the edge. "We could just run off the side of the cliff," he said, rocking more, "and it'd all be over. . . ."

She grabbed his arm, trying to get him to stop rocking. "It's not that easy!" He was rocking less and she relaxed her grip. "It's not easy, Rick." She looked over the edge, shuddering. "We could be crippled, or lose an arm, or a leg, or *both*. . . . Then we'd have to depend on our parents for the rest of our lives. It isn't so simple, to end it."

Slowly, he rocked the bike a few inches away from the edge, to safer ground.

"When you tried it, before, what happened?" he asked, both feet planted on the ground, on either side of the bike.

She turned her wrist over, feeling the scars. Red, ridged scars. "It hurt," she said finally. "And it was scary." She gulped, stroking Timmy. "It really hurt, Rick."

He moved his jaw. "There's other ways to do it."

"No matter how you try to do it," she said, shaking her head, "it's not easy." She moved closer to him. "I remember all the blood. I was so scared! After I did it, I was really, really scared!"

He leaned against her, locking his hands behind her back. "I read in the paper this morning — another kid in that town in Texas . . . Plano, Texas. Then there was a girl who hung herself in a tree in a schoolyard in Los Angeles. . . ."

They didn't speak, listening to the wind and the sound of each other's breathing.

"My grandma had some baby chickens," Lonnie said suddenly. "And one was sick, and I tried to kill it. To put it out of its misery — I'd seen my grandpa do that. I — I hit its head against a post. I kept hitting it, but it wouldn't die. It just kept — kept making all these little chirps." She shivered, remembering. "I was shaking all over. Finally, I took it down and threw it in my grandma's furnace. It was the worst thing I ever did. I — I never told anybody."

He didn't say anything, breathing hard.

"It's *hard*, Rick. To end a life." She lifted Timmy, holding him close to her face and neck.

Rick leaned forward over the handlebars, staring out over the city.

* * *

They sat on his scooter, in the darkness, outside of his house. It looked — different, somehow. Unfamiliar. Rick kept looking — at the lights, the yard — trying to remember what it was like when he was younger. When he hadn't felt this way.

"Every night my mom plays the piano," he said. "For as long as I can remember. She's working on the 'Brahms Concerto in A Minor.'" He paused. "She'll find the photographs in her music."

They got off the bike, arms around each other's waists, Rick staring and shaking his head.

"Maybe, maybe she's already found them." He lowered his voice, almost whispering. "Maybe she's in there right now. By the piano, looking at them. . . ."

"I'm sure she hasn't seen them," Lonnie said. "We can go in, and get them, and —"

"No!" Rick said harshly. "I want her to know the truth. Who this god *is* she's living with. I want *everybody* to know. That house." His smile was very bitter. "The *reality* of that house. What's really going on in there. . . . I'm never going back."

Lonnie sank onto the curb, holding Timmy, patting him. "So, what are we gonna do?" she asked, not looking up.

"We'll go to your house, and —"

"Are you kidding? They won't even let you in the door. Anyway," she hunched over, "they're shipping me out tomorrow. It's —

our last night together." She was up then, clutching her kitten and burrowing against Rick's chest. "Don't let them send me there, Rick! I can't live without you! *I won't!*"

Rick held her shoulders, moving away enough to see her face. "We could go to your garage," he said, "and get in your dad's car. I could hot-wire it."

"They'll catch us again, I know it! Only this time, it'll be worse. They'll put us in juvenile hall!" She slumped against him. "It's hopeless."

Rick rubbed her back before speaking. "I didn't mean we'd *go* anywhere."

She didn't say anything, hugging Timmy as if she hadn't heard him.

"Lonnie?" he asked, his whole body tensed.

Slowly, she climbed onto the back of the scooter. "I — heard you." She looked at him. "There's nothing we can do . . . is there?"

He held her face with both hands, his own face crumpling as he started crying. "I just — I don't want to *feel* this way. I wanna make it *stop*, Lonnie."

Now Lonnie was crying, too, pressing her face against his. "Me, too! I don't want to live without you, Rick. . . ."

He got onto the bike, revving the motor. This time, driving away, he didn't look back.

Lonnie's house was dark. They left the scooter at the sidewalk and slowly walked up the driveway, toward the garage.

"What do I do with Timmy?" Lonnie whispered.

Rick reached over to caress the kitten's head briefly. "Put her down. She won't run away."

Lonnie hesitated. "I can open the kitchen door and put her inside."

"They might hear, wake up."

Lonnie nodding, kissing the kitten and putting her gently on the mat by the kitchen door. "Stay here, Timmy." She glanced back at Rick. "What if a dog comes along?"

"She can climb a tree. Cats can take care of themselves." He paused. "Where's the key?"

Lonnie reached up to the molding over the kitchen door, taking down the garage key. She handed it to Rick who unlocked the door, and slowly pulled it open.

Lonnie hung back. "She'll be out here. Alone in the dark."

Rick put his arm around her. "It's not so dark." He managed a weak smile. "There's the moon."

Lonnie looked up at the sky. "The Big Dipper. Like in your room." She glanced over. "What if we went to my grandma's?"

"She'd call them. They'd come and get us. *Separate* us."

Lonnie nodded. "I couldn't do that to her, anyway. I mean, my grandma. She'd get all upset."

"I don't have any grandparents," Rick

said. "They're all . . . dead." He pulled her closer. "There's no place to go, Lonnie. I'm *drowning*."

Again, she nodded, very slowly. "It doesn't matter, what we do. The whole world's going to blow up soon, anyway."

Arms tightly around each other's waists, they walked into the garage.

It took a few minutes to hot-wire the car. Lonnie sat in the front seat, looking for some music on the radio. She stopped at a heavy metal station, harsh, violent music. The engine started, Rick lowered the hood and came back to the door, sliding into the driver's seat next to her. He closed it softly, then reached over, pulling her into his arms.

"Don't let go of me," Lonnie begged, pressing against him. "Promise you won't let go of me."

"I'll never let go," he said. "*Ever*."

They held each other, hearts pounding, bodies trembling.

"Talk to me," Lonnie said. "Talk about anything. Just talk."

Rick tightened his arms. "Once upon a time, there was a beautiful little girl . . . named Tulip."

She smiled a little, snuggling closer. "Why do you always call me that?"

Rick touched her mouth, his fingers gentle. "Because," he smiled, his eyes blurred by tears. "Because you have the two prettiest lips in the whole world. Because," his hands slid down to her back, "you have a face like a flower." He reached out with one hand and turned up the radio.

Outside, Timmy was curled up on the kitchen mat, asleep, under the light above the door.

Tina sat at the piano, David watching her from the doorway, drinking brandy.

"What do you want to hear?" she asked.

"Whatever you're working on."

Tina picked up the Brahms concerto, not noticing the added thickness. She looked at it, then shook her head, putting it back. "I've been working on this concerto, but I'm too wiped out tonight. How about . . . Debussy? 'Golliwog's Cakewalk'?"

David nodded, slipping into the chair next to the piano, smiling as she started to play.

Chapter 12

Timmy meowed on the doorstep, standing on her hind legs and pawing at the door, hungry for her usual morning milk. Alma, the maid, was on her way up the driveway.

"What were you doing outside, kittycat?" She bent to pat Timmy's head. "Naughty kitty. Naughty girl." She had her key out to open the kitchen door, but paused, hearing music coming from the garage. She listened briefly, then walked over to check. She opened the garage door. Exhaust fumes billowed out, strong enough to almost knock her down. "Mr. Carlson?" she asked, her voice muffled through the hand over her mouth and nose. She took a step inside, then screamed. "Mr. Carlson!" She ran to the car, yanking the door open, seeing Rick and Lonnie's lifeless bodies. She tried to turn off the ignition, but there was no key. Coughing, she ran to the house.

"Help!" she screamed. "Get help!"

Harvey came out through the kitchen door, his shirt half buttoned. "What is it? What's wrong?"

Alma pointed to the garage. "In the car. . . ."

He stared, then realized what she meant and ran for the car. "Call an ambulance!"

He reached inside the car, grabbing for Lonnie and the hood latch at the same time.

"What is it?" Lois shouted, on her way out.

"Open the hood!" He yelled. "Pull the wires!"

She came into the garage, confused. "Harvey?"

"Just *do* it!"

She screamed, seeing him lifting Lonnie into his arms. "Harvey!"

"Pull the wires!" he yelled, carrying his daughter out to the driveway. "Get the motor off!"

She ran to the car, fumbling with the hood catch, hands shaking as she struggled to get it open. She yanked on the wires — any wires — until the engine died, the radio music stopping abruptly. Harvey had come back for Rick, trying to pull him past the steering wheel and out of the car.

"Help me!" he yelled, his voice rasping. "We gotta get air!"

Lois ran to help him, both of them stumbling from the fumes, dragging Rick out of the garage, and lowering him to the grass.

Lois turned, unable to believe that this was happening, focusing on Lonnie, lying pale and limp on the lawn.

"My daughter is dead!" she screamed. She rushed over, crazy with grief. "Harvey, make her breathe! Do something!" She lifted Lonnie to her breast, almost incoherent. "My daughter is dead!" she screamed. *"My daughter is dead!!!"*

The driveway was crowded with paramedics, policemen, and detectives, an ambulance in the driveway and police cars clustered in the street. Harvey and Lois stood with Alma, holding on to each other, staring at the two shapes covered by white sheets, still lying on the ground. They clutched each other, in shock.

"I'll try to make this as brief as possible," a detective said gently, his notebook out. "But I have to ask you a few questions. When did you last see your daughter?"

"I —" Lois spoke like a zombie, still staring. "Last night. About ten. We — had a quarrel." She sagged slightly, and Harvey held her up. "I looked in her room about midnight. She was under the covers."

"The pillows was under the covers," Alma said softly.

"You quarreled?" the detective asked. "She was depressed?"

"A-about going away." Lois struggled with the words. "T-to school."

"We wouldn't let her see Rick," Harvey

said, trying to control his tears. "We wouldn't let her talk to him."

"We — she was so young," Lois said. "We were afraid."

"She's had a lot of trouble," Harvey explained, his voice shaking. "She — tried this before. . . ."

"She cut her —" Lois couldn't go on, touching her own wrists, unable to say it.

David's BMW screeched to a stop at the curb and he ran up the driveway, his eyes wild.

Harvey ran to intercept him. "David — they're gone, David."

David shrugged away from him, heading for the bodies on the grass. He flung the sheet off Rick, bending over him, checking the body. Looking for a pulse, a heartbeat, anything. He lifted Rick's eyelids, looking for pupil dilation, then patted his cheeks, the examination more frantic. Searching for some sign of life, *any* sign of life. Any sign at all.

He held his son's head in his arms, staring at the pale, slack face. Gently, he lowered him to the grass, keeping his hand on his cheek. He nodded at Harvey, too overcome to say anything.

The coroner's van had pulled into the driveway, and two investigators conferred briefly with the detectives.

"It appears to be carbon monoxide asphyxiation," one of the detectives said.

"Both of them?" the older investigator asked.

The detective nodded. "I'd say it was a suicide pact."

"Any notes?" the other investigator asked as they moved toward the bodies.

The detective shook his head. "None so far."

The older investigator bent down on one knee to look at Rick.

"Leave him alone," David said coldly, still next to the body.

"I'm from the coroner's office —"

"Don't touch him!" David lunged for the man, paramedics jumping to hold him back, pulling him away. "My son," he said, his voice anguished.

Neighbors had gathered on nearby lawns, talking in low, stunned voices, the red lights from the police cars illuminating the faces and bodies of the people in the driveway in brief, regular flashes.

The coroner sat behind his desk; David and Tina stood in front of it, numb and dazed.

"Let me see him," Tina said softly.

The coroner coughed. "I'd like to accommodate you, but this isn't a mortuary. It would be much better for you to wait."

"Please," David said. "Let us see him."

"It's so much better," the coroner spoke gently, "at the funeral home. Cosmetically. . . ."

"I'm a doctor," David said, the word feeling flat in his mouth.

"I want to see my son." Tina's voice was slow and steady. "I have a *right* to see my son."

The coroner looked at them, then nodded. "I was only thinking of you." He paused before standing. "This will be very difficult."

Tina started for the door.

"Dr. Morgan?" the coroner said quietly.

David turned back.

"You, uh," he coughed, "understand that we have to do an autopsy on both bodies. To make sure that both deaths resulted from carbon monoxide poisoning."

"Yes," David said, the word almost lost in his throat.

The coroner led them to a curtained-off cubicle. Rick's body was on a table, covered by a sheet. As the coroner pulled the sheet back from his face, Tina slowly approached the table.

She gasped, the recognition worse than she'd imagined. She stared at the gray, waxy face that had been her son, too numb to speak, or even cry.

Philip sat at the piano, playing "Zip-a-dee-doo-dah" with one finger, the notes quiet and fragile. Mournful. He kept playing, staring vacantly at his mother's music folders.

Across the room, Sarah was curled up on David's lap, too bewildered and frightened to cry. David held her, his arms and face stiff. It was as though a bomb had dropped — on the house, on the family — and the ashes were just beginning to sift down.

David sighed heavily. "Philip."

Philip stopped playing, his hands clenching together. "I'm sorry."

"Why can't I see Mama?" Sarah asked, her voice close to tears.

David hugged her. "She's in her room. She needs this time alone."

Sarah huddled closer to him.

"He told me," Philip said. "Yesterday, in his room. I thought he was kidding. I told him he was sicko. I — I wouldn't listen." His hands turned into fists. "Why did he do it? He's ruined everything! Our whole family!"

"I don't know," David said quietly.

"He didn't care about us! He just cared about *her*! About *Lonnie*!"

Sarah started crying. "Daddy. . . ."

"Shhh," David said, soothing her.

"I wish she'd never come home! I wish she'd finished the job the *first* time!" Philip jumped up from the bench, running for the door.

"Philip, wait." David tried to get up, Sarah still in his arms.

"He hated us!" Philip punched the banister, not even noticing the pain jarring up through his arm. "Boy, he really musta hated us all!"

* * *

100

Lois sat on the couch, drinking scotch. It wasn't her first. Or even her second. She kept drinking, while Harvey paced back and forth in front of the couch, his hair and clothes badly rumpled.

Slowly, Lois picked up Lonnie's notebook from in between the cushions, opening it. "She was writing little poems. . . ." She flipped through the pages, stopping at one. "'Look, Mama. See, Daddy. I wrote you a poem on my wrists. I used a razor for . . . a pen.'" She looked up at her husband. "Oh, Harvey. . . ." She stood up, letting the little book fall from her fingers.

Harvey came over, picking it up and looking at the poem. "'I signed my name in blood,'" he read softly, "'But you wouldn't . . . read it.'"

Lois wrapped her arms around herself, unexpectedly cold. "She *wanted* me to read it. She left it out for me to read. She wanted me to stop her."

"'If something happens to me, please take care of Timmy. . . .'" Harvey's voice trailed off and he dropped the book onto the coffee table.

Lois covered her ears. "We have to get out of here! I can't stay here!" She looked around, completely panicked. "I can't look at the driveway, or the grass where she was — I can't get past her room! Harvey, please. Get me out of here!"

"Okay, okay." He put his arms around her. "I'll get the car —"

"Not *your* car!"

"No," he said. "Of course not. They came and took my car."

"The other car," Lois said frantically. "Is it in the garage?"

"I took it out. I parked it at the curb."

"I —" Lois was trying to calm down, to keep the words from running into each other. "Don't ever park the car in the garage, ever again. Harvey, promise me that. *Please*."

He helped her toward the front door. "I promise you, Lois. We won't live here. We'll sell the house."

She nodded, desperately gulping in the fresh night air.

Sarah woke up, screaming. She scrambled out of bed, running, almost falling, across her room, trying to get to the door in the darkness. "Mama! Daddy!"

David was there, scooping her into his arms, carrying her out of the room. "Sarah, Sarah. . . . It's all right now."

She was crying hysterically, clutching him around the neck. "He was here! Sitting on my bed! Rick was here!"

"It was a dream, Sarah. Just a dream." He carried her into the bathroom, sitting her down and washing her face with a warm cloth. Over and over, until she calmed down.

"H-he had the keys to his scooter," Sarah gulped. "And he was laughing, and he asked me to go for a ride."

Gently, David sponged off her hands and

wrists. "Rick would never try to hurt you or scare you."

"Why did he do it, Daddy?" She fell into his arms, crying weakly. "I want Mama."

In the bedroom, Tina was lying — fully dressed — on top of the covers. The room was dark, except for the moon, and a small nightlight in the corner.

David carried Sarah into the room and gently lowered her onto the bed. "Here's Mama."

Sarah moved closer, clutching at her, and Tina lifted one hand to pat her on the shoulder, trying, but too caught up in her own grief to be comforting.

David turned off the night light and sat on the sofa by the window, looking out into the night, Sarah's crying the only sound in the room.

It was just past dawn, the yard and neighborhood quiet except for the birds. Tina crossed the backyard, hunched into her bathrobe, stopping at the pool. Ralph followed her, his tail low, but she ignored him, staring into the still, green-blue water.

The first light was hitting the bedroom upstairs. Sarah was on the bed, twisted up in the sheets, asleep, curled up in a long outgrown fetal position. David was still on the couch, with Philip — who had joined them in the night — sleeping restlessly on his lap.

David let his eyes open, looking around at the wreck of the room. Of the family. Seeing

Tina through the window, he got up, carefully transferring Philip's head to a pillow.

He walked across the dewy grass, stopping a few feet behind her. Ralph whined, wagging his tail, and David patted him absently.

"You have two children up there," he said softly, Tina not moving, "in your bedroom. They're confused, and hurt, and frightened — they need you." He paused. "I need you, too."

She didn't say anything, hunching more, her face very pale.

"We have to hang on, all of us. Together. As a family."

Tina still didn't say anything, her eyes on the water.

"I deal with life and death every day," he said. "I've always been able to perform under stress. I've always been strong, clearheaded, in control." He swallowed. "Tina, I can't handle this alone."

No response.

"I just . . . *can't.*"

The only sound was Ralph whining, rubbing against David's leg.

"We have to make funeral arrangements."

Silence.

"Tina?"

"Do whatever you want," she whispered, her voice quavering.

"You're in this, too. What do *you* want?"

"I want to die," she said.

Chapter 13

The funeral was very crowded, with class-mates, teachers, friends of the families. Throughout the church, the sound of crying was audible, getting worse as the ceremony went on. A mass of numbed grief.

When it was over, the caskets — white, shiny, covered with flowers — went first, Bobby, Jeb, and other friends from school acting as pallbearers, most of them crying.

The families were next, dressed in dark, somber colors, all of them in very bad shape. They left the church, David practically holding Tina up, Sarah and Philip close behind them. Lois, very pale, was helping her mother while Harvey walked behind them, struggling to hold back tears.

Reporters and a crowd of curious onlookers waited outside. Cameras flashed as the families descended the steps, startled by and blinking in the sudden light.

Attendants were holding the doors of the limousines; the two families climbed into separate cars, the doors closing behind them. The other mourners followed more slowly, some crying openly, others quiet and stunned, all of them shattered by the tragedy. They moved back to their cars, headlights flickering on as the procession started.

The funeral procession moved slowly through the streets, the bright sunlight incongruous and almost offensive. People on sidewalks and in front yards stopped what they were doing, watching the cars pass. The procession went by the high school, the campus almost deserted, a few students watching silently from the steps.

Through the Santa Barbara streets, past the hospital, past the video arcade. The drive was slow. Grim.

At the cemetery, the same friends carried the caskets, the families and mourners following. Philip's friend, Artie, all alone, hung shyly, unhappily, at the rear. At the gravesite, the group split, some gathering around Rick's coffin, others around Lonnie's. The Morgans clung to one another, the Carlsons more stiff, the finality of this sinking in for all of them. The faces of the survivors were solemn. Shattered.

The flowers waved slightly in the breeze and there was the sound of a faraway plane crossing the sky. Then, silence.

Tina dropped a small handful of dirt into Rick's grave, her movements mechanical, her face blank. Sarah clung to her arm; Philip cried and hung onto his father. May, David's nurse, stood behind them, stoically trying to hold back her tears.

Now the mourners were gathering on the grass between the two graves, the families sitting on folding metal chairs. Dr. Madsen cleared his throat and stepped forward.

"The families have asked me to say a few words," he said. "I —" He took a deep breath. "I've known Rick and Lonnie since the day they were both born. I was their doctor. I was always concerned about their health, their diets, their immunization shots. . . . I keep thinking about it. Did my responsibility end with their yearly physical exams? Where did I fail? What signs did I miss? I ask these questions over and over again. Looking for an answer. . . . What has happened to our children?" He stopped, rubbing one hand across his face, trying to go on. "When people reach helplessness, they need an act to get them out of it. In an ideal world, a doctor would intervene, or a helping adult." He looked at the silent mourners. "I guess what I want to say to the young people here today and in this community is, suicide isn't the answer. This is not the way to end pain. It only lays it on the broken shoulders of the survivors."

Bobby spoke next, stiff and uncomfortable in front of the crowd, very close to tears.

"I've known Rick since he used to play first base on my T-ball team," he started. "We were in the championships." His hands were shaking and he put them in his pockets, then took them back out. "I remember that day. Bottom of the ninth, bases loaded — and he made an unbelievable catch and won the game. After that. . . ." He swallowed. "Whenever I looked at Rick, I saw a hero."

It was very quiet.

"I wish —" He struggled to keep his voice steady. "I wish I'd realized that heroes can be in trouble. That heroes . . . can really be hurting inside. We haven't been as close as we used to be — I mean, lately. I wish I'd known what was going on. I wish . . . I could have helped."

"Me, too," Jeb muttered, standing with Sherry, both of them staring at the caskets.

As the graveside ceremony ended, Harvey was close to breaking down, crying noisily, in too much pain to control it or cover up. Lonnie's grandmother and Lois started for the limousines, Lois helping her mother across the grass.

"Mama, how do we get through this?" Lois asked helplessly. "How?"

Her mother shook her head. "I don't know. I never expected to outlive my only grandchild." She pulled a scented handkerchief from her pocket, bringing it up to her face. "It's terrible to say, but maybe it would have been easier if it had been some accident. If it had been a car crash. But this. . . ." She was crying now, the handkerchief against her eyes. "It's the most terrible sin there is, Lois. To . . . take your life."

People clustered around the Morgans as

they tried to get into the limousine, being kind and supportive, trying to help. At the other limousine, the Carlsons, by comparison, were cut off. Alone.

David helped Tina up the front walk. She leaned against him, almost unable to hold herself up. A neighbor met them at the front door, holding it for them.

"We've fixed a nice lunch," she said.

"Thanks," David said automatically. "That's really nice of you. Maybe. . . ." He gestured toward Philip and Sarah, then continued inside, helping Tina upstairs.

"Well." Their neighbor, Mrs. Curtis, tried to smile, putting her arms around their shoulders. "Come on, kids. We've got all this good stuff in the kitchen. Can't *believe* all the food that's been brought here today."

Philip twisted away from her, crying and running into the house. Sarah looked up at Mrs. Curtis unhappily.

"I guess . . . nobody's hungry," Mrs. Curtis said.

"I am," Sarah whispered.

Upstairs, Tina ran into the master bedroom and then into the closet, pressing against the rack of clothes. She had her hand across her mouth, trying not to scream, to keep it in. A low moan escaped through her hand and David came into the closet, trying to hold her. She pulled away, crying audibly and pressing against the clothes, almost trying to hide between the layers of skirts and blouses and jackets.

David tried to help her, feeling clumsy and ineffectual. "Hold on, Tina. Hold on."

"Get them out." Her voice was muffled by the clothes. "All of the people. Ask them to go."

"They're just trying to help."

She turned to face him, her face wild and flushed, almost unfamiliar. "Was it my fault, David? *Was it?*"

Sarah sat in the den, slumped in front of the television. The news was on, showing film from the funeral. She gripped her plate, the food she hadn't been able to eat, watching shots of the funeral procession, the caskets. Her family. The Carlsons.

"In Santa Barbara today," the newscaster was saying, "the funeral of two teenagers, victims of a suicide pact. Earlier this morning the city council met with the mayor to discuss a suicide prevention program in city schools."

Sarah closed her eyes, too upset to get up and turn the television off, and started to cry again.

A few days later, David went back to work. It was easier that way. Surgery was precise, complicated work, requiring all of his concentration. It was a *relief* to concentrate on surgery. Not to think about — except that he couldn't. No matter how hard he tried, it stayed with him, no better, maybe even worse.

He walked into his office, grimly determined to concentrate on medicine and nothing else. His day's schedule, his responsibilities . . . and not Rick.

May was sitting at the desk and when she saw him, stood up. "Dr. Morgan." She put out her hand and David clasped it, May unable to speak for a moment. "There's a call for you," she said finally. "She's holding. She insisted."

David stiffened. "Who is it?"

"I think it's — personal," May said awkwardly.

David nodded, heading for his private office. Once inside, he went to his desk, sitting down and looking at the phone. He didn't want to speak to her, but — he didn't have a choice.

Slowly, he picked up the phone. "Hello. . . ." He listened as she spoke, telling him how sorry she was. "Thank you. I appreciate it, I do." He paused, his decision long since made, getting ready to say it. "I can't . . . see you anymore. I hope you understand that. I just can't . . . see you anymore." He let out his breath. "I'm sorry."

It was a week later, maybe ten days after the funeral, and Lois was at her office. She sat in front of her design board, swiftly drawing a shirt design, filling it in with color. She looked at the result, not caring, the pen slipping out of her hand.

Harvey came in, carrying a stock of T-shirt samples. "You wanna go through these?" he asked, his voice extra-jovial and too loud.

She didn't say anything and he spread the samples out across her desk.

"I think we should do the pink and green stripes again next season," he said. "It flies outa here." He pointed to one of the samples. "We could do the stripe smaller, just keep the colors."

Lois stared at her design board without really focusing.

"Lois? You listening?"

"I don't care about pink and green striped shirts anymore," she said, her voice dull and flat. "I don't care. . . ."

Harvey looked at her, then slowly gathered up the samples. "I've got a great idea," he said. "Let's call it a day and go over to Lu's for some Kung Pau Chicken. That stuff knocks your *socks* off."

"I'm not hungry."

"Then we'll just go home." He tried to pull her to her feet. "Get a good night's sleep."

She shook his hand off. "I'm not going home. I don't *ever* want to go home."

He sighed, the manufactured enthusiasm gone. "You can't stay down here again. That lousy little couch —"

"I can't pretend that everything's all right either! I just can't!"

"Lois —"

"Leave me alone!" She headed for the liquor cabinet, grimly pulling out a bottle of scotch and reaching for a glass.

Harvey watched her, then nodded gloomily, sitting down on the couch. He put his face in his hands, listening to the liquid spill into the glass. He sighed, resigned. "Pour one for me."

Chapter 14

It was later and Lois pounded on the Morgans' front door, drunk and angry. Harvey tried to pull her away, but she shook free, still pounding.

"Wait until tomorrow," Harvey said. "We'll call David and arrange something."

"They treat us like we've got a disease!" Lois banged on the door. "Tina won't even talk to me."

"She won't talk to *anybody*," Harvey said, making a conscious effort to keep his voice down. "Not to David, not to the kids —"

"David?" Lois shouted, drowning him out. "Tina?"

The door opened and David looked out at them, confused. He turned on the lights in the foyer.

"What is it?" he asked. "What's wrong?"

Lois pushed past him, into the house. "Tina? Tina, where are you?"

Tina stopped on her way down the hall

from the den, looking very thin in her bath-robe.

Lois rushed over. "Tina. Tina, we've got to talk, we've got to get this out. It's all bottled up and it's just getting worse." She tried to hug Tina, who moved away stiffly. Lois dropped her arms, hurt. "We're friends. We're best friends." She moved closer. "Tina, don't shut me out."

Tina backed up toward the den, shaking her head. "I can't, I can't talk."

"Then, just listen. Because I've got to! I can't hold it in any longer." She caught Tina at the den door, taking her arm. "I'm going crazy, Tina! Everybody avoids the subject. Nobody even mentions her *name* — except in the papers. All the sordid stuff on the news. . . ." She turned toward Harvey and David, somewhat off-balance. "Lonnie! My daughter, *Lonnie*. She was alive. She was a person. She existed — she's not some terrible disgrace."

Harvey came over, touching her arm. "Come on, honey. You've had too much to drink."

Lois shook away from him, following Tina into the den. Her friend, Tina.

"If I can't talk about my daughter and what happened, what *do* I talk about, huh?" she asked all of them. "What do I see when I close my eyes at night?"

David came in last, after listening at the bottom of the stairs to make sure Philip and

Sarah were still asleep. "Sit down, Lois. Harvey."

Harvey looked at him helplessly, not sure how to explain. "She keeps blaming herself. But you know, Lonnie was a hard kid. From the very beginning. . . ." Awkwardly, he sat down, hands twisting in his lap. "She used to lie in her crib and hit her head against it. Thump, thump, thump until she finally fell asleep out of sheer exhaustion." He stopped, the memory too painful for him to go on right away. "The other night I thought I heard it. Thump, thump, thump. I woke up and — and I was so happy. I thought she was in her crib. For a few minutes there," he smiled a little, remembering, "I thought — I was so happy and so relieved. . . ." His voice trailed off.

It was quiet in the room, none of them looking at any of the others.

David shifted his weight. "Can I, uh, get you something?"

"No, no." Harvey shook his head, just as uncomfortable. "We've had — enough." He looked at the floor, away from his wife.

"She knew," Lois said. "Even then, when she was a baby. She knew that, that" — tears were welling up in her eyes — "no matter how hard she cried, or how long she banged her head on her crib, it was useless. There was no way to get my attention." She covered her eyes, the tears spilling out. "I just want her back again! I want them to bring her to me, my baby, wrapped in a flannel blanket. I want my baby again. I want to hold her" — she folded her arms, as though rocking an infant — "and touch her face, and her baby hands and feet and ears. . . . I want another chance, to be a good mother."

Tina started for the door, unable to listen.

Lois moved to intercept her. "Tina, we *need* each other. We can help each other."

Tina pushed her away. "I can't." She stared at her friend and some of the emotion broke out. "I look at you and I see Lonnie! If it hadn't been for Lonnie, I'd still have my son!"

"Do you know that?" Lois asked, her own anger flaring. "How do you *know* that? You had all these foreign exchange students wandering in and out of your house and your own son was the most foreign one of all!"

Tina covered her ears. "Don't!"

"He was lonely and isolated!" Lois shouted.

Tina slapped her across the face, almost hysterical. "Get out of here!" she screamed. "Get out of my house!"

David grabbed her, holding her body against him, trying to calm her down.

"Do you think you're suffering more than we are?" Lois asked. *"Do you?"*

David sighed. "For God's sake, Harvey. Take her home."

"Home?" Harvey asked, losing his own temper. "Who has a home? You want to go to our home? You want to walk past our garage? Your *son* is the one responsible, *he* hot-wired the car!"

"Make them stop, David!" Tina screamed, hands clamped over her ears. "Make them stop!"

"Harvey, get out of here!" he ordered. "Go!"

"We're all in this together," Lois said desperately. "They were our children! We're *friends*!"

"No!" Tina pulled away from David, backing up toward the wall. "We're not. I don't ever want to see you again in my life. Never! Don't call! Stop sending notes! Stop driving past this house! Just — go away! Disappear! It was your fault! It was *all* your fault!"

"Don't say that." Lois started crying again. "Please don't say that. Oh, Tina. Tina, please don't say that."

Harvey looked at David. David, his childhood friend. His best — "David," he started.

"Did you hear her?" David yelled. *"Go!"*

Sarah, all alone, roller-skated on the back terrace. It was getting dark and she had turned on the outside lights, practicing the same maneuvers over and over again. She'd set up her radio on a lawn chair, and it was playing Top 40 music, Sarah trying to skate in rhythm with the songs. She kept skating, going into a spin and an awkward leg lift. She tried again, performing only for Ralph, lying a few feet away, watching her with his muzzle resting on his front paws.

"Okay now, Ralph," she said. "Watch close. I'm going to try it again."

Upstairs in Rick's bedroom, David watched his daughter's forlorn little figure skate around the terrace. Then he turned, studying the room. He walked into the dark-room, touching pieces of equipment he didn't understand, seeing some eight-by-ten-inch pictures of Lonnie still pinned to the drying line.

He went back into the bedroom, pausing at the bookshelves, reading the titles. Poetry, philosophy, comparatively little science. He read on, realizing — maybe for the first time — what his son had been all about.

"What are you gonna do with his records?" Philip asked, at the door.

David looked up, blinking quickly to cover his emotion. He pulled the cardboard box of records over the bureau. "I'll take them to the hospital," he said gruffly.

"Maybe" — Philip hesitated — "I should keep 'em."

David looked irritated. "You don't like Rick's music. You never did."

"Rick said they grow on you."

"Well, you're not Rick!" His father snapped.

It was briefly silent, Philip leaning against the bookcase, hurt.

David started pulling shirts from the bureau, putting them into an empty box.

"Yeah, well —" Philip gulped, somewhere between yelling and tears.

"There are a lot of people down at the

hospital who would *enjoy* them," David said, packing shirts.

Philip came over to the box, picking up a jersey with black sleeves. "I always wanted this shirt. From the Who tour. . . ."

"Philip," David said, only half paying attention, "your mother sees you in that shirt and it'll tear her apart. Stop thinking about what you can *get* and —"

"He was my brother!" Philip shouted, his eyes filling with tears. "He would have wanted me to have that shirt!"

David looked at him, suddenly realizing his other son's pain. "I'm sorry," he said quietly. "I'm not myself anymore. Take the shirt. Of course you should take the shirt." He gestured around the room. "Take anything you want here."

Philip slammed over to the door. "Forget it."

As Philip left, David sank down onto the edge of the bed, his face in his hands. How could everything fall apart so quickly? One minute, the family was — and then — he let himself slump back onto the bed, exhausted. The room seemed to be closing in. Rick's books. His records. His clothes.

David reached toward the light panel, slowly pressing a switch. Above him, the stars lit up. Beautiful stars, bright and shining. Rick working for hours. Making constellations, beauty. Looking up at the stars, David started crying.

"Oh, Rick," he said to the ceiling.

Chapter 15

A few weeks had passed, life limping along. Struggling. Harvey hurried down the aisle in the factory shipping room; Lois followed, very upset.

"I think you should be there," she said.

Harvey shook his head, walking faster. "I'm not going, Lois."

"It would help us, I know it would."

"It's *private*."

"You've been avoiding anything unpleasant or difficult for sixteen years!"

Several workers glanced up and Harvey flushed.

"I don't want to discuss my personal life with a lot of people," he said through his teeth, emphasizing each word in turn.

"It *isn't* private," Lois said, her hands on her hips. "Our lives have been in newspapers all over the country! I think we have to say something, get it out."

Harvey strode into his office. "You go, Lois. You don't need me there."

"But I do!"

He closed the door, and with it, the subject. Lois put her hand on the knob, ready to protest further, than gave up, starting for the exit.

She went to the meeting at the school that night; the auditorium was crowded with parents. Very nervous, she had dressed much more conservatively than usual, wearing a simple dress and almost no makeup. She stood in front of the group, feeling herself perspiring.

"I —" She adjusted the microphone, her voice seeming too loud. "I've never spoken in public before."

Dr. Madsen nodded at her reassuringly, sitting in the front row. The faces in the audience were sympathetic, waiting for what she had to say.

"Dr. Madsen asked me to come here tonight to speak to all you parents. At first I said no. . . ." She licked her lips, wishing that she had a glass of water, wishing even more that Harvey had come with her. Been brave enough to come with her. "I-I didn't think I would be able to get up on my feet in front of a group of people. But," she swallowed, her throat very dry, "I have to talk. I think it's important to talk about what happened to our family."

The auditorium was very quiet; parents leaned forward, listening intently.

"If my husband died," Lois went on, "I'd

be called a widow. There's a name for that. There's no name for what I am now. No name for what we have to live through." Tears, the thing she had dreaded the most, were threatening and she had to stop, taking several deep breaths to control herself. "There were so many signs of what our daughter — Lonnie," she corrected herself, "was going to do. She'd even *tried* it before, and she talked about it a lot. She wasn't interested in seeing any of her old friends." Lois twisted her hands together, remembering the signs, remembering the way she had brushed them aside. "She was hostile, impulsive. She wasn't interested in school. She seemed so — hopeless, and I guess —" Aware that her voice was fading, Lois made a conscious effort to speak more loudly. "And we kept thinking it would pass. . . ."

After Lois' speech, Dr. Madsen stood up to address the group, Lois standing next to him.

"We've got to set up workshops in all our schools," he said, "where a therapist can actually talk to the kids. Show them that there are other ways to deal with these overpowering emotions."

A man in the audience raised his hand, then stood up. "The whole town's in shock," he said. "All the stuff in the newspapers. Everybody's scared that more kids are going to — that they might . . . do it, too."

Now a woman stood up, on the other side of the auditorium. "When you observe these signs — suicidal behavior" — she shifted her weight, trying to find the right phrases — "say your kid makes some dramatic changes in eating habits and sleeping habits. Withdraws from friends, becomes obsessed with death. What do you do?"

"You get help!" another woman called out.

"Well, okay," the first woman agreed, sounding tentative. "But how do you know if children are really distressed, or just trying to manipulate their parents to get what they want?"

"You don't know," Lois answered. "Just don't take that chance."

It had been several weeks since it happened. Sarah and Philip were in the den, slouched in chairs, watching television. These days, they seemed to spend most of their time that way.

A man was being interviewed. A young guy, handsome, wearing jeans and a well-fitting T-shirt. He was enjoying the interview, smiling at the camera.

"I guess I've killed about a hundred people," he said. "All sizes and ages. I've lost count."

The camera angle widened, including the woman who was interviewing him.

"And you're still smiling?" the woman asked. "You've been convicted, you're waiting on death row."

The man shrugged and laughed. "It was

good for a laugh. I loved it." The camera moved in, close to his eyes, wide and deranged. "Figuring out ways to dispose of bodies, cutting them up —"

Sarah reached out, snapping the set off.

"Hey!" Philip protested, forgetting his TV dinner. "I want to see this. This guy's really a creep."

"I can't watch," Sarah said. "He's too terrible." Her stomach hurt and she put her dinner tray aside, untouched. "This stuff looked better on the picture," she said, looking at the food.

"Look, turn it back on." Philip indicated the television with his fork.

Sarah shook her head. "Why can't my friends come over?" she asked suddenly.

Philip stopped eating. "Mom can't handle it."

"Probably nobody would *want* to come over here anyway." She slouched lower in her chair. "How long's it going to be like this?"

"I don't know," Philip said, also slouching, but trying not to show it.

Sarah kicked at the floor with one sneaker. "Hillary called. They're having this welcome party at school for all the mothers. She wants me to come and bring Mom."

"Dad'll go with you."

"It's for *mothers*."

"Yeah." Philip took his tray back, staring down at it without much appetite. "But if you don't have a mother, your father can come."

"I *have* a mother!" Sarah said, crying.

Philip scowled. "Crybaby."

"Rick told you not to call me that! It just makes me cry more!"

Angrily, Philip got up, turning the television back on. "Rick, Rick, Rick. That's all I hear!"

"I wasn't crying about Rick!"

The interview was over and, angrier, Philip turned the television off. "You're crying about Mama and your stupid" — he mimicked her voice — "school party."

Sarah burst into harder tears. "I was crying about . . . all the *killing*! On television, everywhere. So much killing," she whispered.

Chapter 16

Days passed and Philip felt like everyone was half living them. He sure was. Getting up, eating breakfast, going to school — everything took so much effort.

He stood in the foyer, putting books into his knapsack. He didn't bother bringing his baseball glove or a football anymore. Sports didn't seem to mean as much.

A car horn beeped outside and he opened the front door. His ride. Slowly, he started across the lawn, adjusting the knapsack on his shoulder.

"Hurry, Philip!" Artie yelled out the car window. "We're going to be late!"

Upstairs, Tina watched him from her bedroom window as he ran for the car. As usual, she was in her bathrobe, her hair severely pinned back. She kept looking, even after the car was gone, looking, but not really seeing anything.

* * *

The bell had rung and everyone was hurrying to class. Philip was chasing after Artie, but then he stopped, seeing the bulletin board. There were several posters on the board, about the suicide workshop and suicide prevention. He stared at them, unable to move.

A hand came onto his shoulder and he flinched.

"I do the same thing," Bobby said, behind him. "I can't ever get past this board."

Philip turned, keeping his head down in case his eyes were red.

"What's your first class?" Bobby asked.

"Um, American history . . . something," Philip muttered, not looking up.

"Come on." Bobby kept his hand on his shoulder. "I'll walk you."

Philip nodded gratefully.

David parked his car in front of the school the morning of the welcome party for mothers.

He glanced over at Sarah. "Ready?"

She shook her head and pressed back against the seat, obviously petrified. "I thought I wanted to come, but now I don't," she said weakly.

"Come on, honey. I'll be with you." He opened his door, beckoning to her with his right hand.

"You'll — stay right with me?" she asked, hanging back.

"Like glue," he promised.

She slid out of the car after him, clinging to his hand as they walked toward the school.

"Is it all right?" she asked uneasily. "Your coming instead?"

He nodded, holding the door for her.

The corridors were decorated with brightly colored paper streamers, bulletin boards covered with flowers and leaves cut out of construction paper. There was a large handmade sign in the front entrance hall that said WELCOME MOTHERS. Sarah gripped David's hand, not going any farther.

"It's okay," he said. "Come on."

There were mothers and daughters wandering together through the halls, in and out of classrooms where handicrafts and class projects were displayed, papers with high marks pinned up on the bulletin boards and walls.

A large mural, obviously handpainted by students, spread across one of the walls in the corridors and Sarah stopped in front of it.

"One of them is me," Sarah said shyly. "You have to guess."

David looked at the mural, walking the length of it once, examining the bright paintings. He stopped and pointed at one girl. "Here."

"How could you tell?" Sarah asked, both surprised and pleased.

"The socks." He touched the pink polka dots on the drawing of the girl's socks, then pointed down at the bright dots on Sarah's anklets. "And the ponytail," he said, giving hers a gentle yank. "And the eyes. . . ."

Self-conscious, Sarah looked at the painting. "I look like a real geek."

"No, you don't."

Seeing her, several girls ran over.

"Sarah!" one said.

"Hi, Sarah," another one chimed in. "Come on."

Sarah looked up at her father, not sure if she would be allowed. "Is it okay, Daddy?"

He smiled. "It's okay."

She smiled back, her whole face lighting up, and ran off with her friends.

Tina sat at the kitchen table, drinking a cup of tea. She was wearing her bathrobe, but she had combed her hair into a neat bun.

David stood at the counter, fixing himself a bowl of ice cream. "Now that Sarah's back in school," he said, shaking the spoon, the ice cream sticking, "maybe it'd be good for you to start helping out once a week as a class mother."

Tina smiled slightly, sipping her tea. "Maybe."

"Work's the answer." He closed the ice-cream carton, putting it back in the freezer. "Getting involved again. When I'm in the middle of surgery, there's no time to think of anything else."

"I wonder," Tina said, holding the tea cup

with both hands, "if it can ever be normal. Like it used to be."

David came over to the table, leaning over to touch her face with one hand. "You know what I'd like? I'd like to hear you play the piano. I really miss hearing you play."

"I don't know if I still can," Tina said, her voice so soft that he could barely hear her.

"Of course you can. It'd be good for you."

She nodded slowly and stood up, heading for the living room. She stopped, flexing her hands experimentally. "I'm very rusty."

"Go on," he said.

She crossed to the piano and sat down, her hands flexing more easily. David stood in the doorway, holding his ice cream, happy to see her looking more animated. More like herself.

Tentatively, Tina touched a few keys, then played a few chords.

"Sounds good," David said.

Tina smiled, both hands testing chords. "Quiet from the peanut gallery."

"You know what I'd love to hear? Brahms. The Brahms concerto you were working on."

Tina's hands stopped and he was afraid that he had pushed too hard, too quickly. But she reached for the stack of music over the keyboard, going through it, pulling out the Brahms. She looked at the first page, took a deep breath, and started to play.

David leaned against the doorway, smiling, listening.

Playing with more confidence, Tina reached up to turn the page and the music stopped abruptly as she saw the pictures. David and the Woman. Smiling. Embracing. Tina stared at the photographs, her hands frozen on the piano keys.

"Honey?" David asked, behind her. "What's the matter?" He came over, stopping in shock as he saw the pictures. "Tina —" He couldn't find his voice. "Tina, it was nothing. You've got to believe me, it was —"

Tina shook her head, eyes riveted to the picture of David and the Woman kissing. "Why are people so cruel to each other?" she asked softly.

Chapter 17

Upstairs, Tina grabbed David's clothes from the closet, flinging them on the floor, moving in a frenzy. David stood just behind her, trying to explain.

"I — I don't know what to say." He ran his hand through his hair. "I go over and over it and I don't — know what to say. . . ." He sucked in a deep breath. "The woman —"

"I don't want to know about the woman!" Tina shouted, throwing the last of the clothes onto the floor. "I don't *care* about the woman!"

"It's over," he said. "It didn't mean *anything*."

"It means something to me!" She whirled around to face him. "*It meant something to your son!*" She ran past him to the bathroom, grabbing his shaving equipment and lotions from the medicine chest and throwing them onto the floor. "Take all of it! Don't leave anything!"

Sarah came to the doorway, rubbing her

eyes sleepily, frightened by the yelling.
"Mama?" she asked. "Daddy? What's the
matter?"

"Nothing!" David snapped, then recovered himself. "It's nothing, honey."

Tina stormed into the bedroom, dropping
the toilet articles onto the pile of clothing.
"Don't you tell her that! Don't lie to her!"

"We're having some problems," David
said calmly, Sarah staring at them, looking
frightened and confused. "We're going to
work them out."

"Tell her the truth!"

"Go to bed," he said, ushering Sarah to the
door. "I'll be in to kiss you good-night in
just a minute."

Hesitantly, Sarah started for the hallway,
looking back at her mother. Not understanding.

David winked at her, putting on a happy
smile. "Go on now."

Sarah went down to her room and David
closed the door.

He turned. "She's a little girl, Tina. Don't
hurt her more than she's been hurt already."

"Oh." Tina yanked his shirts from his bureau drawer. "The great Dr. David is an
expert on child-rearing? Tell me about it.
Tell me how careful you were with Rick!"
She started on his sock and underwear
drawer. "You kept him hopping, didn't you?
No time to relax, no time for anything friv-
olous — like friends! He had to study more
and do more and know more!"

"I never stopped him from having friends," David said defensively.

"He was *too busy* for friends, *too busy* expanding his vocabulary! *Too busy* being perfect! *Too busy* trying to be his dad!"

"I —" David blinked quickly. "I wanted a lot for him. I thought I was doing the right thing."

"It was all your ego! You wanted Rick to be another *you*! 'Your son.'" She shook her head, gripping some of his undershirts in her hands. "There were never any real feelings. That's why you like being a surgeon so much — your patients are anesthetized. You can talk to them, and they don't have to listen!" She turned to face him completely, her whole body trembling. "He *worshipped* you, David. I did, too! All these years, building this home and this family. I bought all of it!" She imitated his voice. "'Love, respect, honor, truth, kindness, beauty.' I fell for it. I thought you were — I thought *we* were —" She stopped, trying to keep from falling apart. "You betrayed me, David. You betrayed all of us!"

"I love you!" He tried to hug her. "Tina, I love you. Don't *do* this to me!"

She pulled away from him. "Don't touch me! Don't you *ever* touch me!" She backed up more, shaking uncontrollably. "It wasn't just Lonnie and Rick in that car — we were there, too. You and me!" She sank against her dresser, covering her face with her

135

hands. Then, she looked up. "Please take your clothes out of my room."

They looked at each other and then David bent down to pick up his things. Something cracked inside and Tina swept her arm across the chest, sending framed pictures of the family crashing to the floor. Baby pictures, wedding pictures, school pictures — a whole family history — crashing and breaking.

"Tina!" David crouched down among the shattered glass, trying to gather the pictures up. "Our kids, our *lives*!"

"Take all of it!" she screamed.

Lois and Harvey sat in a bar, the only customers left. A quiet, wailing song was playing on the jukebox and Lois stared at her glass, at the dregs of the scotch.

Harvey glanced at his watch. "It's almost one." He looked at her. "Ready to ramble?"

Lois laughed, the sound harsh. "You know what I was thinking? We got married because I was four months pregnant. . . ." She went on before he could interrupt. "It's true. I used to pray that I'd lose the baby — can you imagine that? I'd say to myself, 'I will not have this baby!'" She hunched over her drink, the memory hurting.

"Lois —" Harvey started.

"She must have really wanted to be born," Lois said, ignoring him. "She must have wanted life *so* much, before she had it. . . ."

Harvey shifted uncomfortably, not speaking.

"We've never had a marriage," Lois said, more tearful than bitter. "Our relationship was based on our problems, problems we had with Lonnie. *That* was what we shared. As long as we had the hysteria about what to do with her, we were okay. We didn't have to face — the rest of it. The emptiness." She looked across the table at him, her eyes bright with tears. "So, here we are, Harvey. You're there, and I'm here, and what's in between?"

"Well — we have the business, Lois," he said uncertainly.

"The business." She laughed shortly. "I don't care about the business — I don't want it anymore. You can handle it without me."

"Don't be crazy! You're the designer!"

"You'll hire somebody." She picked up her glass, finishing what was left of her drink. "I was thinking. . . . I'd like to travel. I always had this thing about the pyramids." She nodded. "I want to see the pyramids before I die."

Harvey reached across the table, catching her hands in his. He held on tightly, desperately. "You *love* the business. You eat and *sleep* the business."

"No," she said. "I don't."

Her voice was so flat that he let her hands drop, bringing his own hands back to the edge of the table.

"What about the work you've been doing?" he asked finally. "With the suicide prevention workshops?"

She shrugged. "You can take over. You'd be good at it."

"We've . . . been married sixteen years," he said, awkwardly. "That has to mean something."

"That's what's so terrifying," she said quietly. "It doesn't —" Her voice was even lower and he had to strain forward to hear her. "It doesn't mean anything at all." She slumped forward, her head on her arm.

"Come on, Lois." He helped her up. "I'm taking you home."

Mechanically, Tina prepared breakfast for the rest of the family — what was left of the family — dark pockets of sleeplessness under her eyes. Sarah and Philip were at the table, very quiet as they ate their cereal.

"Are you . . . coming to school with me this morning, Mama?" Sarah asked, aware of her mother's unhappiness.

Tina shook her head vaguely. "No."

"You said you might."

"I — can't."

David came in, fixing his tie, trying to make it seem like a normal morning. He moved to the stove to pour himself some coffee, Tina carefully avoiding him.

"Hey, Dad," Philip said with his mouth full. "Aren't you gonna eat?"

"I'm in a hurry." He stirred his coffee, then put the mug on the counter, untouched. "I, uh, have to run down to the hospital and check out some X rays."

"I could come down and help out at the office after school," Philip offered. "You know, like Rick did. . . ."

"Rick was programming the computer," David said stiffly. "It's very technical. We can't take a chance on making an error on somebody's medical history or medication." He bent to give Sarah a quick kiss, not noticing Philip's shoulders sag. He turned, giving Philip a clap on the shoulder, then looked at Tina. "I'll — see you tonight?" He headed for the foyer without waiting for her reaction.

Tina waited at the stove for a second, then went after him, catching him at the front door.

"You can come back at noon and get your stuff," she said, keeping her voice low. "Nobody will be here."

"Tina —"

"I'll figure out something to tell the kids —"

"Tina," he said.

"I can't even look at you! I can't . . . look at you."

"All right," he said, defeated. "Whatever you say."

Chapter 18

Tina drove to the Carlsons' house, parking at the curb. She had thrown on some jeans and a sweatshirt, and her eyes felt red and swollen. But probably, here, it wouldn't matter.

Slowly, she got out of the car, looking at the house, and at the garage. She steeled herself and walked up to the front door.

Lois, at the kitchen window with a cup of coffee, saw her and lowered the mug.

"Harvey...." She moved toward the front door.

"Huh?" He lowered his newspaper. "What is it?"

Lois opened the front door and, a few feet away, Tina stopped. They looked at each other, then Tina hurried over.

"Lois," she said, helplessly, and the two women embraced.

Later, they drove out to the beach, parked well above the water, and got out to lean against the car. There were some boys on the beach, racing on motorcycles, on a make-shift track of hard-packed sand. The soft whine of their scooters and the crashing surf were the only sounds.

"I think you should try to call him, Tina," Lois said. "Try. He loves you and you love him and you have to talk — *at least.*"

Tina shook her head, her arms folded tightly against the cool wind. "I can't. There's nothing left."

"You have a *family* left. That's a lot more than I have."

Tina bent down, picking up a shell frag-ment, rubbing it between her thumb and forefinger. Then she sighed, tossing it away. "Nothing's the same," she said. "Nothing looks the same, nothing even *tastes* the same. I drink a cup of coffee — and I can't taste anything." She inhaled deeply. Twice. "I can't even smell the sea. It's all flat now, and lost and sad — and over."

"You still have two children, Tina. You've got to start paying attention to them. You can't just shut yourself off."

Tina glanced up at her. "What about you?"

Lois slumped back against the car, her face empty. "I haven't got anything *to* save. Harvey and I are at the end of the line."

Tina straightened up, listening.

"*You* still have a chance at something," Lois went on. "You still have a chance to talk to your kids, to listen. I can say that because

I blew so many chances with Lonnie. And I can't get any of them back, ever."

Tina nodded slowly, not speaking. Not having to speak.

That night, trying to make things better, Tina suggested that they grill hamburgers outside, giving Philip most of the responsibility. She'd explained that David was working late, not ready to go any further.

The sun was going down and she sat at the redwood picnic table with Sarah, trying to lift the mood of unhappiness, too unhappy herself to be very successful.

Across the yard, at the grill, Philip scooped some hamburgers up, dropped them into buns, and carried the big plate over to the table.

"Wait," Tina said, getting up to help.

"Stay down," Philip said, his voice a little deeper than usual. "I got 'em."

"I'm not hungry," Sarah said.

"Don't worry, you'll love these." Philip put one on her plate. "Rick taught me. You put cheese in the middle and —" He made an okay gesture, indicating that the result was primo. He gave his mother a hamburger, then sat down to start on his own.

"Mama?" Sarah asked, sounding tearful. "Give me a hug." She reached over, cuddling against Tina, who did her best to respond.

Philip hunched over his hamburger, concentrating on eating.

"Mama?" Sarah asked. "What was the first word I ever said?"

" 'Light.' You said," she mimicked a tiny little voice, " 'Light.' Every time we passed a light bulb, you'd reach out and try to touch it."

Sarah smiled, picturing that. "Was I cute?"

Philip reached across the table for the catsup. "You looked like a wet rat."

"I did not! Anyway," she settled back against her mother, "you can't remember that far back."

"I saw pictures." He grinned, cupping his ears to make them stick out. "*I* looked like Dopey. Big ears and everything."

"N-no," Tina said, struggling to join in and make all of this seem normal. Happy. "You didn't. You were beautiful." She picked up her iced tea, blinking several times. "All of you were beautiful."

Philip laughed. "Are you kidding? *I* saw pictures. My head was lopsided." He made a grotesque face, head tilted, features twisted. "I was drooling."

"Was I smart?" Sarah asked.

Tina tried to laugh, feeling it catch in her throat. "Very smart. Quick and bright. Alert. From the very beginnning. When I first held you in my arms and looked down at you —" She stopped, remembering the other baby she had held.

"What about me?" Philip asked.

Tina managed a flimsy smile. "You were a terror. Especially when you learned to

walk. I couldn't turn my back one second. . . .
I'd be changing Sarah and you'd run into
the bathroom, climb up on the sink, and get
in the cold cream! Rick was always trying
to keep you out of things. . . ."

There was an awkward silence, and Sarah
climbed onto Tina's lap.

"Remember?" she asked, and started a
pantomime with her hands. " 'Two little
blackbirds, sitting on a hill. . . .' "

" 'Fly away, Jack,' " Philip sang in a low,
froggy voice. " 'Fly away, Jill.' "

"Let *me*," Sarah protested and continued
the pantomime. " 'Alice, thin as a toothpick,
head just like a tack. . . . Alice, where art
thou going?' "

" 'Upstairs to take a bath,' " Philip sang
in a high, squeaky voice.

" 'Alice jumped into the bathtub, pulled
out the stopper plug. . .!' "

" 'Oh my goodness, oh my soul! There goes
Alice down the hole!' "

" 'Poor Alice,' " Sarah sang sadly. " 'Ah-
na-men. . . .' "

This time, the silence was horrible, the
song bringing back memories nobody wanted.
Philip pushed his plate away, resting his
head on his arms. Sarah hung limply against
their mother, Tina seeming just as limp.

"Why do we say ah-na-men instead of
amen?" Sarah asked finally.

Tina swallowed. "When Rick was little, he
couldn't pronounce it and he grew up saying
ah-na-men."

144

Philip lifted his head, tears running down his cheeks. "We just copied. . . ." Crying harder, he ran toward the house.

Tina slumped down, not having enough energy to go after him. "You didn't eat your hamburger," she said vaguely, her words lost as Sarah started crying, too.

Chapter 19

Tina stayed outside for a long time. Coming inside, she walked through each room, looked around for a few minutes, then turned off the lights. The bedroom was particularly alien. It felt cold. Lifeless.

She went into her bathroom, staring at her reflection in the mirror. Pale, tired, eyes red. She picked up her brush and was running it through her hair when she noticed a pill bottle overturned on the sink. Slowly, she picked it up. The bottle was empty.

Empty! She dropped it, running through her bedroom to the hall.

"Philip!" she yelled. She threw his door open, but the bedroom was empty. "Where is he?!"

Sarah came out of her bedroom, sleepily confused. "What's wrong?"

"Where's Philip?"

"I don't know. I thought he was in bed...."

Bed. Tina spun around, running toward

Rick's room. "Philip!" she screamed, bursting into the room.

He was at Rick's desk, his head resting on his arms, very still.

Tina ran to him, grabbed his head, pulled it up. *"Philip!"*

He opened his eyes groggily, blinking in the light.

Tina was crying, half mad with fear. "My sleeping pills!"

"Only . . . only three," he mumbled.

She slapped him across the face as hard as she could. "Damn you! Just damn you!" She slapped him again. "How could you do that to me? How could you?"

"I —" He tried to block her away. "I'm okay." His head flopped down.

"Quickly," Tina said to Sarah, who was standing behind her, crying. "Get your father's exchange. Tell him to meet me at the hospital! Call Lois, ask her to come and get you. Hurry!"

Sarah ran out of the room.

"I don't need to go," Philip mumbled, "to the hospital. I'm all right."

Tina pulled him to his feet, giving him a rough shake. "I can't believe you! I can't believe anything you say! Who can trust you, if you'd do a thing like this?" She shook him again, her anger at him, and at Rick, exploding at once. "Just damn you! Damn you to hell!"

She pulled him down the stairs, Philip's movements clumsy. Drunken.

"You better be sure next time to take enough pills!" she said, her voice trembling almost as much as she was. "You could do brain damage, you know!"

"I could just . . . shoot myself," he said, stumbling over his feet.

"You know where there's a gun?" She pulled him, half falling, toward the front door, Ralph lumbering out of their way.

"Maybe. . . ."

She dragged him outside. "When do you plan to do it?"

"Tomorrow," he said vaguely. "Maybe tomorrow."

"In the head or in the heart?"

"I dunno!" he shouted.

"You gonna do it here? So I'm the one to find you?!"

"You always paid attention to Rick!" Philip yelled, too weak to pull away from her. "He always got the attention!"

"All your brother got was *death!*" she yelled back. "He's *dead. Over!* He had this gift, this miracle! Life! And he took it! Nobody has that right! To take a life! To throw a life away before you even start it!"

"Stop . . ." Philip crumpled against her, crying. "Mama. . . ."

"You think I'm brutal?" She yanked the car door open. "Well, suicide is brutal! And ugly! And painful! So *think* about it next time!"

She pushed him into the car, then slammed around to the driver's side. She was shaking, crying so hard that she couldn't get the key into the ignition. She gave up, her crying closer to whimpering.

"Why did you do that?" she asked. "Why?! Why don't you just take a gun and shoot *me*!"

Philip was sobbing, almost incoherent. "I feel awful! There were times — I used to wish he was dead! He was always better than me, and Dad liked him more, and —"

"It wasn't you, Philip. You didn't make it happen. You *couldn't*!" She pulled in a shuddering breath, struggling for control. "Rick was the one who made it happen. He's the one who did it, and it's such a terrible, terrible. . . ." She sank forward against the steering wheel. "It's such a terrible waste." She stayed against the wheel, crying quietly. "It's wrong, Philip. It's just — unacceptable. It's wrong."

They didn't speak for a few minutes, both of them crying.

"Mom?" Philip asked shakily. "Do you — want me to drive?"

She stared at him. "*You* took the pills! You're doped! Besides, you don't know how to drive." She paused. "Do you?"

He nodded, hesitantly. "A . . . little."

"You know how to drive! You probably snuck the car out."

They looked at each other and suddenly started laughing, Tina pulling him over into a tight hug.

"Oh, Philip," she said against his hair. "I

don't know anything about my kids. I don't know anything."

It was two hours later and Tina walked down the hospital corridor, David next to her.

"They pumped his stomach," David said. "They just want to keep him overnight for observation."

"Everything's falling apart." Tina hugged herself, trying to stop the trembling. She glanced at her husband, feeling several different emotions at once. Powerful emotions. "What have we done to them? To our kids?"

"Tina. . . ." He rubbed a tired hand across his eyes. "Calm down. We've got to figure out a way to help him."

"I don't know what to do, David! What are we supposed to do?"

"Whatever it is, we will," David said.

When they went in to see him, Tina was somewhat more composed. Philip was lying in the bed, eyes shut, and Tina crossed over to him.

"Philip?" she asked softly.

He opened his eyes, looking weak and sick.

Automatically, she straightened his covers. "I'm sorry I was . . . so rough on you."

"I know," he said, his voice rasping.

"I'm just" — her throat tightened — "I'm so angry at Rick."

"I am, too," Philip whispered.

David approached the bed, slowly bending down to his son. They exchanged a long look and David grabbed him, hugging him close.

"Philip, don't do this again." David pulled him still closer. "Please don't ever do this again."

They hung onto each other, surprised, and even overwhelmed, by the love between them.

Chapter 20

The next morning, Tina and David sat in Dr. Madsen's office.

Tina perched on the side of a chair, very jittery. "I keep thinking about Rick," she said. "That night. Why didn't I go to his room? Why didn't I check on him? I play it over and over. I see it in my mind, and I'm trying to get to his room, and my legs are like rubber."

"Last night, you got to his room," David said.

Tiny shook her head. "It's not the same. Philip only took three pills. He didn't mean — he wasn't trying to —"

David glanced at Dr. Madson. "How do we know that?"

"Well." Dr. Madsen moved his jaw. "Three pills doesn't mean suicide, but it's definitely a cry for help." He leaned forward, dropping the pen he was rolling between his hands. "David, Tina — you're a high risk family.

You have to face that. Suicide is a *learned* procedure."

"Is this going to be our *life*?" Tina asked. "Trying to keep our children alive? Is that what you're saying?"

Dr. Madsen shook his head, but only slightly. "What I'm saying is that you need professional help. You're going to have to deal with the present, with immediate problems. The next few years are going to be comparable to an Outward Bound survival test. There are people who can help you — schools, churches, public service organizations. But you're going to need tremendous courage and," he paused, "unity."

Tina and David looked at each other.

After the meeting, they walked to the elevator, staying a couple of feet apart.

David broke the silence. "There's no way to bring Rick back. We've got to concentrate on the living." He moved a little closer. "We have Philip, we have Sarah. We have a *life* together."

Tina didn't say anything.

"I'm sorry, Tina. I'm just so sorry." He started to reach for her, but paused. "I-I don't know if you can ever love me again, but — please. Try."

Slowly, he reached for her hand, and she didn't pull away.

A couple of days later, Lois spent the afternoon in her room, packing her suitcase. She packed swiftly, eager to leave.

Harvey came to the door, watching her pack, his expression unhappy. "Your cab's here."

She nodded. "I'm ready." She zipped up the suitcase. "I'll send everyone postcards from Cairo."

"I wish you'd let me take you to the airport."

"I hate good-byes," Lois said briskly. "You know me." She picked up the suitcase. "I hope — you'll be friends again with David."

Harvey shrugged, ignoring that. "You'll call from the airport?"

She nodded.

"What about your stuff?"

She smiled sadly. "I don't want it, Harvey."

"You worked for it! All these years — harder than me! It's *yours*."

"Give it to charity," she said. "I want to travel light."

"Oh. Well." He followed her out into the hall. "The lawyers will work out a fair arrangement for your share of the business. It's fifty-fifty all the way."

"I trust you," she said.

Another silence.

"Well," he said.

Lois smiled painfully. "We never have much to say to each other, do we? Unless it's about T-shirts."

They laughed softly.

Harvey reached out to carry her suitcase. "You laughed. That's the first time you've laughed . . . since Lonnie."

They started down the stairs.

"That's another thing we'll always have to talk about," he said, very solemn. "Lonnie. Even though she's gone, we still have her. A part of her. What she gave us."

Lois nodded, her face tightening.

Outside, Harvey held the taxi door for her.

"You know I'll miss you," he said, his hand on the window frame. "I don't hafta say it."

Lois looked down at her hands, at the wedding ring. "Say it."

"Lois, I will miss you. I will miss you every day, in every way."

She nodded, tears in her eyes. "Me, too. I'll miss you."

"I *do* love you," he said. "I just didn't know how to show it."

She nodded again.

As the cab pulled away, he lifted his hand in a small wave.

Lois looked back at the house. The FOR SALE sign out front, the yard, the driveway, the garage. She looked at Harvey, returning the small wave. He was very alone, standing on the curb. Very vulnerable. She watched him walk back across the yard, pick up Lonnie's gray kitten — now a cat — and carry it into the house.

Tina stood in the kitchen, holding the phone, listening to the exchange student begging to see her about his class schedule.

"I'm sorry," she said. "I just can't meet you today. Maybe tomorrow we can go over your schedule, but today . . . today I'm spending with my children." She paused, listening. "Yes, with my daughter. And later, I'm going to play tennis with my son. Okay, we'll talk tomorrow." She hung up the phone, starting for the living room, where Sarah was practicing her trumpet.

"Sounds good, Sarah!" Tina called out. "Just keep going." She walked into the living room, seeing Sarah strain at the mouthpiece, struggling to play the notes. Any notes.

Tina sat down at the piano to accompany her, playing a simple Russian folk song, "Dark Eyes." Sarah tried to follow her, but gave up, sitting on the bench next to her.

"Mama?" She rested the trumpet in her lap. "You're not going to get a divorce, are you?"

Tina stopped playing. "No."

Sarah nodded, relieved. "I was scared there for a while. Hillary's mother and father are getting a divorce, and Tommy Cirolia's. I hate it when you and Daddy fight."

Tina leaned over, brushing a kiss across her hair. "It's a hard time . . . for all of us. Your daddy and I aren't perfect. We have lots of problems."

"Is that what the doctor means when he says it's gonna be hard for all of us to — survive what happened to Rick?"

Tina nodded. "Yes. But we will. And we'll do it *together*, as a family."

Sarah thought about that. "How long will it take?"

"I don't know."

"I do," Sarah said. "It's gonna take forever."

Tina nodded.

Chapter 21

It was suicide prevention meeting night; Harvey, Dr. Madsen, and a psychologist were leading the group. Harvey was still pretty new at this, but he was trying.

A teenage girl was speaking, her voice shaking as she stood in front of the group. "My mother c-committed suicide. Does that mean — I'm going to?"

The psychologist shook her head. "Suicide isn't inherited. We're not bound to follow in the footsteps and disasters of our parents. *Learn* from your mother. Her death doesn't have to be in vain. It can teach you how to live."

"But if I felt really bad —" The girl stopped. "I mean — what should I do?"

The psychologist nodded. "There's a number you can call, and there's always somebody there who is trained to help you. Who'll understand. Who'll listen. You don't have to tell anything you don't want to." She looked around at the group. "I know it's hard to believe, but pain does pass. It does."

Dr. Madsen spoke up. "I think a lot of people have romantic views about suicide. Let me tell you something. It isn't romantic. It's the end of a life. It's *death*."

It was Harvey's turn to speak, and he swallowed nervously. "I had this dream last night. I was walking on this gray, cold beach with my little girl. She was about three. I turned to look at something, and when I looked back . . . she was gone. She'd disappeared. And I didn't look for her. I just stood there, numb. I didn't even report her missing, I just — I think that's what happened in real life." He had to swallow again, to try and control the emotion that was bubbling up. "What I want to say is, I'm not a professional, but I'll always listen. If anyone wants to call me. . . ."

Chapter 22

Harvey stood on the factory loading dock, checking some crates on their way out for shipment. He heard someone in the alley and turned to see David.

"Hey," he said, not sure how to react. "David."

David reached up, grabbing his arm. "Come on. "You're coming to dinner."

"Oh, no." Harvey tried to pull away. "I've got a bunch of invoices I have to go over and—"

David punched him lightly on the arm. "Shut up and come on. Tina's made your favorite — grilled chicken with salsa and tortillas."

Harvey hesitated.

"Come *on*," David said.

They ate in the dining room, candles lit, casting a golden light over everything. It was a happy meal, everyone talking and laughing, almost like old times.

"I'll tell you," Harvey said to Philip and

Sarah, "your dad and I were inseparable until your mom come along."

Tina blushed.

"One look at Tina and I knew old Hot Shot had met his match." He grinned. "He was the movie star. I was the jerko. All the beautiful women fell for him — I couldn't get one of them."

"Except for Lois," Tina said softly.

Harvey nodded. "Except for Lois."

It was quiet in the room, everyone avoiding everyone else's eyes.

Sarah stood up, going to the kitchen. "I gotta get something."

Harvey smiled then. "All the good times we had in this house. Thanksgiving. . . ."

"Oh, and Christmas," Tina said. "Lonnie and the kids hanging their stockings, and you all sleeping over."

Harvey nodded. "Every Fourth of July."

"Remember the time we had the chili bake-off?" David asked, laughing.

"Yeah," Philip said. "Rick got so sick he almost died!"

The silence was back then, abruptly.

"He was in bed for a week," Tina said, her voice quiet, but strong. "He turned pale if you even *mentioned* chili after that." She laughed, and the others joined in, the moment over.

"Happy birthday to you," Sarah sang from the kitchen, coming in with a birthday cake, the candles glowing.

The rest of the family joined in. "Happy

birthday to you, Happy birthday, dear Harvey —"

Harvey stared at them, almost falling off his chair with surprise.

"Happy birthday to you!" They finished, and Sarah put the cake down in front of him.

"It's my birthday!" Harvey said. "I forgot all about it." He shook his head. "Holy cow, it's the sixth. I was writing checks all day and I never even —"

"Make a wish!" Sarah said. "Hurry!"

"Oh — yeah." Harvey was completely flustered. "A wish." He closed his eyes. "I wish. . . ."

"Not out loud!" Sarah reminded him.

"Oh," he caught himself, "yeah." He closed his eyes, making a silent wish. "Okay." He blew the candles out in one breath, and everyone clapped.

Philip let out a screeching whistle between his pinkies. "Way to go!"

"What did you wish?" Sarah asked, in spite of herself.

Philip laughed. "He can't tell."

Sarah leaned on the coffee table, staring at the cake. "There were forty-six candles. Forty-six! We had to buy five packages." Dreamily, she touched a few of them. "I wonder if *I'll* ever have that many candles on a birthday cake. . . ."

Harvey patted her hand. "You will," he said, very solemn. Then, he looked around at everyone. "Thank you, for my birthday party."

Tina stood up. "It's not over yet. Everybody in the living room before we cut the cake!"

Philip jumped to his feet, moving into action. "Now," he announced, "right here on our stage, in person, playing A, B, and D flat —"

"No, Philip!" Sarah ran to get her trumpet. "Playing 'Dark Eyes'!"

Tina sat down at the piano; Sarah went to her music stand and adjusted her mouthpiece, preparing for the performance.

David and Harvey came in, smiling, and stood just inside the doorway.

"And now," Philip said, "playing 'Dark Eyes' . . . the Trumpeting Morgan Sister leading the Morgan Family Band!" He picked up his harmonica. "Give 'em a big hand, everybody!"

David and Harvey applauded as Tina started to play, and Sarah lifted her trumpet to her mouth. Philip began with a quick improvisation; Sarah joined in, blowing rusty notes. But Tina and Philip kept going, and Sarah gradually warmed up, the blasting notes turning into a melody.

As Harvey smiled, sitting down on the couch, David moved over behind Tina, and rested his hand on her shoulder. David smiled at everyone, smiling at the eager life in their faces. All of them happier. All of them surviving.

Afterword

Surviving is not a true story. But it might as well be. Every year, hundreds of thousands of teenagers attempt suicide. Some of them succeed in killing themselves. Many fail, but do permanent damage to their brains or their bodies in the attempt. For its victims, suicide is *final*. For friends and family left behind, the suicide of a loved one is devastating.

If a friend or someone you know is thinking of suicide, you can help. Take your friend's threats seriously. The American Association of Suicidology recommends the following: "Don't be afraid to talk about it. Your willingness to discuss it will show the person that you don't condemn him or her for having such feelings. Ask questions about how the person feels and about the reasons for those feelings. Ask whether a method of suicide has been considered, whether any specific plans have been made, and whether any steps have been taken toward carrying out those plans. Don't worry that your discussion will encourage the person to go through with the plan. On the contrary, it will help him or her to know that someone is willing to be a friend. It may save a life.

"Don't turn the discussion off or offer advice. Be a concerned and willing listener. Keep calm. Discuss the subject as you would any topic of concern.

"Get help. Suggest a call to a Suicide Prevention Center. Or suggest that the person talk with a sympathetic teacher, counselor, clergyman, doctor, or other adult he or she respects. If your friend refuses, take it upon yourself to talk with one of these people for advice on handling the situation. In some cases you may find yourself in the position of having to get direct help for someone who is suicidal and refuses to go for counseling. If so, do it. What at the time may appear to be an act of disloyalty or the breaking of a confidence could turn out to be the favor of a lifetime. Your courage and willingness to act could save a life."

Teenagers who think they may commit suicide usually give silent messages for help to the people around them. You may not pick up on them if you don't know what they are. There are nine warning signs of suicide. If someone you know shows any of these signs for several weeks, or if they show two or more signs for just a few days, talk to a trusted adult quickly. It's important to get help as soon as possible.

SUICIDE WARNING SIGNS

- **Expressing suicidal thoughts** or a preoccupation with death.
- **Giving away prized possessions**, making out a will, or making any other preparations for death.
- **Change in sleeping patterns** — either sleeping much too much, or much too little.
- **Change in eating habits** — losing or gaining a lot of weight.
- **Change in school performance** — suddenly getting poor grades, cutting class, dropping out of school activities.
- **Change in social activities** — dropping friends, spending more and more time alone.
- **Personality changes** — nervousness, agitation, or outbursts of anger. Or, on the other hand, apathy and carelessness about appearance, health, and hygiene.
- **Abuse of alcohol, drugs;** or other self-destructive behavior, such as getting into a lot of accidents or taking life-risking chances.
- **A previous suicide attempt.**
  — *Reprinted with the permission of* Co-Ed *Magazine.*

WHAT TO DO

- **Discuss it openly and frankly.**
- **Show interest and support.**
- **Get professional help.**

What if you are the one thinking about suicide, and no one seems to care?

There are people who want to help. Call the Suicide or Crisis Prevention Center in your area. There are more than 200 such centers in the United States. You can find their numbers in the white or yellow pages of the phone book, or by calling Information. Or if you live in a small community and there is no Suicide or Crisis Prevention Center in your area, call the Emergency Service of a Mental Health Center; there is a Mental Health Center in almost every county. Again, you can get the number in the phone book or through Information. Another number to call is 1-800-621-4000, toll free. This is the National Runaway Switchboard, which deals with every type of crisis, 24 hours a day.

The people you'll talk to at these centers are people you can trust. They will listen to you and they will keep your conversation confidential. They want to help you.

If it takes a long time for someone to answer the phone when you call a Crisis Center or if you hear a busy signal, *don't give up*. Keep trying until you get through — there *is* someone there who wants to talk to you. Sometimes, these centers are forced to use an answering tape to handle all their calls. If you hear a tape when you call, *don't hang up*. Listen to what the tape says; there is almost always another number you can call if you need to talk to someone right away. If there is no other number to call, leave a message on the tape. The person who calls you back will ask for you by your first name. If you're not there, they won't tell your parents who's calling, but they will leave a number so you can call them back.

Finally, you can call the local police (by dialing 911 or the Operator) or just go to a hospital. The emergency room of a hospital is always open, 24 hours a day.

If you're feeling like there's no way out, talk to someone about it. You can get help.

If you would like more information about suicide prevention, or if you would like a list of the Crisis Prevention Centers nearest you, write to:

The American Association of Suicidology
2459 South Ash
Denver, CO 80222

The National Institute of Mental Health
5600 Fishers Lane
Rockville, MD 20857

The National Mental Health Association
1021 Prince Street
Alexandria, VA 22314

For further reading:

Cain, Albert C., ed. *Survivors of Suicide.* Springfield: Charles C. Thomas, 1972.
Cottle, Thomas J. *Golden Girl: The Story of An Adolescent Suicide.* New York: Putnam Publishing Group.

Giovacchini, Peter. *The Urge To Die: Why Young People Commit Suicide.* New York: Macmillan, 1981.

Hyde, Margaret O., & Elizabeth H. Forsyth. *Suicide: The Hidden Epidemic* (gr. 9-up). New York: Franklin Watts, 1978.

Klagsbrun, Francine. *Too Young To Die: Youth & Suicide* (gr. 7-up). Boston: Houghton-Mifflin, 1976. (Revised edition, New York: Pocket Books, 1984.)

Kleiner, Art. "Life After Suicide." *Highwire*, Summer 1982, p. 48-53.

Mack, John E., and Holly Hickler. *Vivienne: The Life and Suicide of an Adolescent Girl.* Boston: Little, Brown & Co., 1981.

Madison, Arnold. *Suicide and Young People.* New York: Clarion, 1978.

McCoy, Kathleen. *Coping with Teenage Depression.* New York: New American Library, 1982.

McKnew, Donald H., Jr., M.D.; Leon Cytryn; M.D.; and Herbert Vahraes. *Why Isn't Johnny Crying?* New York: Norton, 1983.

Mead, Cheryl. "Why Teenagers Are Killing Themselves." *Co-Ed*, September, 1984 p. 67-72.

Zusman, Jack, and David L. Davidson, eds. *Organizing the Community To Prevent Suicide.* Springfield: Charles C. Thomas, 1971.

point®

Other books you will enjoy,
about real kids like you!

☐	MZ43124-2	**A Band of Angels** Julian F. Thompson	$2.95
☐	MZ40515-2	**City Light** Harry Mazer	$2.75
☐	MZ40943-3	**Fallen Angels** Walter Dean Myers	$3.50
☐	MZ40428-8	**I Never Asked You to Understand Me** Barthe DeClements	$2.75
☐	MZ41432-1	**Just a Summer Romance** Ann M. Martin	$2.50
☐	MZ42788-1	**Last Dance** Caroline B. Cooney	$2.75
☐	MZ33829-3	**Life Without Friends** Ellen Emerson White	$2.75
☐	MZ43437-3	**A Royal Pain** Ellen Conford	$2.75
☐	MZ42521-3	**Saturday Night** Caroline B. Cooney	$2.75
☐	MZ40695-7	**A Semester in the Life of a Garbage Can** Gordon Korman	$2.75
☐	MZ41115-6	**Seventeen and In-Between** Barthe DeClements	$2.50
☐	MZ41823-8	**Simon Pure** Julian F. Thompson	$2.75
☐	MZ41838-6	**Slam Book** Ann M. Martin	$2.75
☐	MZ43013-0	**Son of Interflux** Gordon Korman	$2.75
☐	MZ33254-6	**Three Sisters** Norma Fox Mazer	$2.50
☐	MZ41513-1	**The Tricksters** Margaret Mahy	$2.95
☐	MZ42528-5	**When the Phone Rang** Harry Mazer	$2.75

Available wherever you buy books ... or use the coupon below.

2053